A WRITER'S

NOTEBOOK

A WRITER'S NOTEBOOK

Everything I Wish Someone Had Told Me
When I Was Starting Out.

by

John Scherber

SAN MIGUEL ALLENDE BOOKS

San Miguel Allende Books
San Miguel de Allende, Guanajuato, México

ACKNOWLEDGMENTS

Any book starts as an idea, and by its completion becomes a joint effort.

Thanks to my wife, Kristine, for editorial and critical help.
Cover Design by Lander Rodriguez
Cover Photo by Michael Stetzler "John Scherber at Pine Street, 1964."
Web Page Design by Julio Mendez
Interior Book Design by Kristine Scherber

ISBN 978–0–9832582–8–5

San Miguel Allende Books
San Miguel de Allende, GTO, México
www.sanmiguelallendebooks.com

ALSO BY
JOHN SCHERBER

NONFICTION
San Miguel de Allende: A Place in the Heart

FICTION
The Devil's Workshop
Eden Lost

(The Murder in Mexico series)
Twenty Centavos
The Fifth Codex
Brushwork
Daddy's Girl
Strike Zone
Vanishing Act
Jack and Jill
Identity Crisis
The Theft of the Virgin
The Book Doctor

(The Townshend Vampire Trilogy)
And Dark My Desire
And Darker My Wrath

CONTENTS

PART I

PART II

Author's Note

Excerpts from a few of these chapters have appeared in abbreviated form in my blog, *An American Voice in México*, and in the San Miguel Writer's Conference Blog.

INTRODUCTION

The purpose of this book is a simple one. It is to share with other writers, and with readers who would like to become writers or are merely curious about the process, the lessons I've learned over fifty years of both writing and being unable to write. It is the story of revelations and insights I gained from a personal journey over what felt at times like quicksand beneath my feet, or resembled a labyrinth in the gloom ahead. Although it covers many aspects of the craft, it does not purport to be exhaustive or complete. The reader may come up with questions I haven't considered, and may not even be able to answer. But what I have included is everything I wish someone had told me when I was starting out. My goal is to keep the careful reader of this book from making some of the mistakes I made, such as having writer's block for thirty-seven years.

Writer's block, like other less serious bumps in the road, which are too many to list, is something we do to ourselves, and it is within our power to undo it and move on. Because of my ordeal in working through that process, and finally reappearing on the other side as a productive writer, this book was written from the heart.

There are as many ways to write as there are writers. Only one of them is good for you, and that will be the one that enables you to work continuously and productively. I am not a guru—in fact, I disrespect most gurus—I am only a practical working writer of extensive experience. My way will not be the best way for you in its entirety, but it includes ideas and practices that can help you in critical ways. While many of them will help you avoid pitfalls, few of them are shortcuts.

Many of the insights in this book were obtained only at great cost. Your task in reading it is to approach these ideas with an open mind and try them out. Feel free to reject anything that doesn't feel right. Anything that *does* feel right will be like having the wind at your back and a clear view forward. I can only offer what I've learned after making what seemed like all the possible mistakes in this field more than once.

Today the world of publishing is in great flux, and will continue to be as new technologies and marketing systems contend with the old ways of printing and selling books. Much of this is good news for both writers and readers, although from a distance it can look like a minefield, which it will easily become for the unwary or uninformed. I have included some chapters on the current state of self-publishing, and methods to get you started if that's the route you decide to take. Still, the reader will be wise to factor in the rapid pace of change and to verify any factual information of mine that he decides to act on to see that it is still current.

I am primarily a writer of fiction, specifically mysteries, although I write nonfiction in both book form and magazine articles, and other genres as well. I have framed this book, however, to apply to all types of fiction because the rules of the publishing business that require books be labeled as one genre or another gloss over the process of writing, which does not vary greatly from one species of book to another. Most of it will also be helpful in nonfiction, which may differ less from fiction than its name suggests. A writer in any genre can face the same problem of how to get started at the top of an intimidating blank page, or how to create settings that become active characters in the story. How to persuade his living characters stand up and speak. Every fiction book needs a savvy treatment of pace, plot and character to succeed. It must be sensitive to language and diction, which charts a route into the reader's mind. These are only a few of the issues I address in this book.

Like any of the arts, writing is essentially a journey over rugged terrain. If you are taking the proper degree of risk, much of this terrain will be uncharted on every project. Even with a reliable guide, it is mostly a solitary task, and the only competition you will encounter is the writer you were yesterday. The route travels through a world without external limits; you will never bump the edges, because there are none. You can go as far and as fast as your energy, drive, and imagination will take you. Any limits you discover in the process will be self-imposed, and part of the task must sometimes be to act as your own therapist. Fortunately, self-imposed limits are the easiest kind to remove, but you must be able to recognize what they are first. If you encounter a task you feel you cannot do, the first question to ask yourself is who is telling you that you can't.

We'll begin with a bit about my background, which may be unusual, but it illustrates some of the common pitfalls awaiting an incautious beginner, a condition for which I was the poster child. You will also find issues in these first two chapters, and later, of course, that could have come from your own struggle.

PART ONE

THE CRAFT OF WRITING

1.

WHERE DO WRITERS COME FROM?

In a larger sense, most writers are born from active readers; readers who more than once reached the end of a page and said to themselves, why can't I do that? I might not do it in the same way, but my way might even be better.

This was how it started for me, since I grew up reading. At ten years old I was devouring about 125 books a year. Perhaps it was an escape, but if it was, it placed me firmly in a larger and more complicated world than most of my friends inhabited.

When I was in high school, the smell of artist's oil paint also lured me like a siren's song. In my mind at that point, I planned to be a writer, not an artist, but I *needed* to paint too. In the studios of painter friends I'd watch in awe as they shoved paint around on their canvases. Oil paints don't smell now the way they did then; they've been cleaned up. We listened to jazz as we drank sweet Portuguese wine in a wicker-covered bottle. Like the crazy Bohemian studio life of that time, the paint has all been airbrushed, sanitized.

When I wasn't wishing I could paint, I was aching to be an archaeologist. You could also use a paintbrush to wipe away the dust and mold of ages from a skull. I borrowed a book from the library called *Lost Worlds*. I re-borrowed it so many times that I wore it out. My favorite photo in it was of the archaeologist Howard Carter peering through the first small opening into the tomb of Tutankhamen in November of 1922. He had worked for years in the Valley of the Kings, and more than skill or insight, it was persistence that got him to that point. Some would call it stubbornness.

Eighty-seven years after that photo was taken, I stood in that steaming tomb in the Valley of the Kings myself. October provided no relief. King Tut is still there, unwrapped and resting quietly. The unrelenting passage of time has not treated him kindly. Still, you can lean your head to within inches of his and speak to him, as I did. It had taken me a long time to get there, and it meant a lot to me, but he was unresponsive. This would not have been his idea of how to spend eternity.

Like those dreams of mine, high school dreams rarely hold up. Your best girlfriend is not the one you marry, or if you do, it may not last. If it does last, you sometimes wonder what other connections you've missed. Where is Cindy now, or Rebecca? The college you chose didn't teach archaeology, or if it did, it offered a single course about Indian mounds in Illinois, not Egypt. Someone told you that all the royal tombs there have already been discovered, so don't bother.

Find something else to do. Get a real job. Why are you special?

In college I became a real writer for a while, alternating short stories with theater and film reviews. Like painting and archaeology, it was something I became passionate about. So I did it for a while, and it almost seemed like a real job at times. Three years after graduation I ran off the rails after writing two bad novels and was unable to write anything more than a grocery list for *decades*. I sometimes felt like my mind was in prison, and I didn't know who had the key.

High hopes or pipe dreams? You stumble and you get up again. The writer was still in my mind and heart somewhere, struggling to find his voice. Year by year it grew fainter, trapped in solitary confinement.

Howard Carter started out as an illustrator in the early years of the twentieth century working among the monuments of ancient Egypt. His persistence in looking for that royal tomb may have something to tell us, because he would've gone on as long as there was funding.

Eventually I took up art again, much later, and became a competent painter, although I didn't quit my day job, my *real* job.

Then, on a painting trip to Taos, New Mexico, in a new century, a new millennium, a fragment of a mystery story came uninvited into my head as I snaked my way down through the mountains. A young woman is coming to have her portrait painted, and she thinks it may be an occasion for a little more than that with the painter, whom she finds far too attractive. The artist, whom I named Paul Zacher, finds her attractive as well, but in the studio, his standard of discipline prevails, otherwise it's only chaos. He's on the job, one he takes seriously. A choice misunderstanding between them follows.

What I knew by the time I wrote this scene was that being a painter really does make you see things differently. Wouldn't that also help if you were a detective? Because, on that very assumption, Paul Zacher is drafted into taking a closer look at a murder.

Yet, he's more reluctant than flattered. At

thirty-five, Paul is most comfortable staying with what he does best. But like the lure of the things he never did, that he walked away from, that he might have done better if he'd only stayed with them longer, he digs into this case. And then he digs some more.

If you've read this far, it's probably no surprise that Zacher's murder case involves some archaeological relics; Mayan ceramics. He also gets a bit of help from his Méxican historian girlfriend, and from a retired homicide detective they know.

Some of you will be way ahead of me here, because I was a bit farther down the road into Taos before I realized I had finally put it all together. All the high hopes and pipe dreams came back to me in a rush. I was a writer again, after thirty-seven years of dead silence, and I was a painter too, painting, through the steady hand of Paul Zacher, pictures that went far beyond what my modest real skills could ever create. In my book, I was the crime-solving sleuth with the hot girlfriend, and I was young, and nothing was impossible. Writing this book was more fun than anything I'd ever done before, and a book that's fun to write is usually also fun to read.

I titled it *Twenty Centavos*, and it became the first of a series of eleven mysteries featuring Paul Zacher, the painter turned detective, and his friends.

They're mostly set in San Miguel de Allende, México, a classic colonial-era town in the mountains that plays host to about 10,000 expatriates. It is also the town where I live today.

Suddenly I was writing fiction again, bringing to it the experience of more than twenty-eight years in business, which was an unexpected resource. A reader once asked me if Paul Zacher was based on me. I said, "No, but I *am* Paul Zacher and all of those characters, and I am none of them."

2.

THIRTY-SEVEN YEARS OF SILENCE

That's how it started. That experience of coming
into Taos was the way back into writing. I like to
suggest that I hold the world record for writer's block:
thirty-seven years. If Guinness has never called me
to account for saying this without documentation, it
must be because they don't have this category in their
book. Perhaps they should. I'd like to see my name at
the top of their page.

Things started out reasonably enough. Let's
take a closer look, because periods of writer's block
are common not only in people starting out, but in
experienced writers as well. In high school I discovered the power of words—I was articulate on the
page and off. Teachers encouraged me even as they
tried to contain me. I sensed the tension, and many
years later it still comes up. Don't rock the boat,
remember your place. In college I wrote for the
literary magazine, then edited by Garrison Keillor,
and became theater and film critic for the college

newspaper. Some time in my junior year I started a novel called *Crickets and Fog*.

The title said it all. It was dense with atmosphere, (an essential element), and it had a fairly normal (I felt at the time) plot involving an incestuous relationship between fraternal twins. My professor at San Francisco State, Herbert Kubly, a winner of the 1956 National Book Award for *An American in Italy*, proposed that I give it an Isis and Osiris theme. Ancient myths, he suggested, can provide a deeply resonant vocabulary of plots. I'm not sure whether this would have helped me or not. In any case, the girl ended up at the bottom of the swimming pool, as her twin brother sank to the bottom of a complex stew of self-contemplation. Whether he learned anything from it or not, I don't know, but I do know that I didn't.

The next novel was set in the San Francisco of the mid-sixties, and at this distance I can no longer remember the title. I wish I didn't remember any of it, but sometimes memory cooperates and sometimes not. It concerned a group of hip people laying about smoking grass while they uttered profound statements. I hope now that the profound statements weren't italicized, but I don't recall. Anyway, how did you italicize with a Smith-Corona portable electric typewriter? The occasional romantic interlude came to nothing, but a couple of scenes with near misses on motorcycles boosted the pace. Both books were unpublishable and, worse, I couldn't deny it.

I awakened from this futile dream at the age of twenty-five with the sense of being at a fork in the road. In one direction I could continue to write bad novels, spending a year at each one. Suddenly I sensed I could no longer waste that amount of time on projects that promised to be worthless. I hung up my typewriter.

For a year or two I didn't know who I was, but that didn't lead me to any insights about why my writing hadn't worked. From the perspective of now, so many years later, it's clear to me that I was too ego-involved. For my books to fail suggested a failure of myself at the deepest level. But I still missed writing. Being a writer was embedded in my psyche, and its absence left a void I couldn't fill any other way.

About ten years after I quit I had an idea for another writing project, and sitting down to start it, found myself gripped by the most visceral discomfort I'd ever known. It was like physical panic, and I realized it was the fear of failing again. I couldn't write, no matter how much I thought that completing something decent, no matter how short, would atone for my initial stumbles.

So it went. Several more times over the years I had the same bruising experience. Why I retained any hope that I could ever write again, I can't explain.

In the interim I'd taken up art, painting landscapes for a gallery in Minneapolis and another in Dallas. I painted a series of abandoned family farmsteads in the Midwest, collapsing barns, ruined cars and pickups rusting into the weedy soil. Remembering my art studio friends, I had always wanted to paint, but thought I probably couldn't. Perhaps proving that was wrong opened the door to something more. I still read a lot, as I always had, and several years earlier I'd started reading detective novels. Out of this emerged some ideas of what elements went into a good mystery. Why did some work better than others?

What followed was the experience in Taos that I described above.

By late August after that trip I'd completed the initial draft of that first mystery, *Twenty Centavos*. Afterward, I revised it three times and began the second book in the Paul Zacher detective series.

What had happened? Over the years I'd never shared my agonies about writing with the people around me. Most were a little surprised, but not shocked, that I had suddenly produced a mystery. It held no special meaning for them.

But something critical had changed. I was sixty years old and I had recovered a skill I had lost in my mid twenties—if I'd even had it then. How often does that happen? On impulse, I looked up *recovery* on the Internet, and found it only applied to alcoholics and drug addicts. It offered no term to describe my experience.

A simple answer came to me over time—it happened because it didn't matter. Of course, it did matter, since I'd done it, but it didn't matter in the same way it had so many years before. My recovery was not about me and my deep but battered need to be a writer; it was about the book itself. I had already had what success I was going to have in business. I was a decent, but not great, painter. I had nothing else to prove, and to have written no books at all, beyond the two novels that I'd long ago burned, would not have diminished me.

I believe this is what made it possible: *the ego part was gone.*

The emerging task was no longer to write— it was now to hold back the stream of books that I didn't realize were dammed up inside my head, to get them down coherently, and to write them well. The book that began on a downward slope through the mountains into Taos, *Twenty Centavos*, was the first of eleven Paul Zacher mysteries. In the seven years that followed that week in Taos in 2005, I wrote eighteen books.

The silence had ended, the dam had broken, and that journey of recovery through those eighteen books is what made *this* book possible and meaningful.

3.

GETTING STARTED

You write a letter to your daughter, a college freshman in Iowa in her first year of living away from home, and next you write one to your father, a retired barber living in Prescott, Arizona. You mistakenly switch the letters in the envelopes, and by the time you realize that might have happened, they are already on their way. If the news they carry is much the same, why is this a problem?

The answer is that we approach different people with different styles of communication. You have not written the same letter to both your family members, even though each one contains an essentially similar packet of news. The reason is that in your approach to different people in your family, *you* are presenting different aspects of yourself, and it's discoverable in your voice on the page.

Although a book is much larger and more complex than any letter, it nonetheless must be designed for a particular reader. Otherwise it seems to float unattended in a vague kind of undirected space, much like an eighteenth century balloon experiment. I approach this issue by trying to imagine my target reader as an individual person before I start writing. Suppose I am planning my first mystery, titled *Twenty Centavos*, as I did on that Taos trip. First, I know that my reader is slightly more likely to be a woman, on the simple basis that more women than men are readers. This tells me up front that my characters, detectives and villains though they are, must be emotionally accessible. Women especially want to be able to get into the heads of characters, to see why they act as they do. Men are more attracted by pace, but many male readers also need the same sustenance of strong character development. Together, their interest is less likely to be sustained by a book based on rapid pace and quick-draw kinds of action where character is secondary or undefined. Although, make no mistake, pace is critical in almost any book. The trick is to balance it with rewarding and clearly developed characters.

We know that mystery readers as a group love a series with the same core players. They long for an alternative reality that, once they find it hospitable, they can revisit again and again. Writers love this feature too, because each reader is an automatic prospect for buying the next book. I think of most of my books, certainly the mysteries, as entertainments. This is not to disparage them, because writing an effective entertainment is difficult, but they are not considered "literary" fiction by the literati, most of whom do not write much themselves.

My detective character, Paul Zacher, is a thirty-five year-old artist who lives in México. He is brought into the action, as I have said above, because he sees things differently. So now we have art as a secondary subject in the book, and indeed, there is a fair amount of painting going on. People interested in art can get involved in painting technique, which is handled in a lively manner. The commodity at the root of the crime is a collection of counterfeit Mayan ceramics of superb quality, which introduces the additional subject of Mesoamerican antiquities. The foreign setting with a warm climate adds the spice of travel as our target reader curls up on the sofa across from a mellow fire in a Massachusetts January. Soon she has forgotten the cup of cocoa on the lamp table near her shoulder. The task of the writer is to make her forget everything else about her life at that moment.

Now we can flesh out our reader a little further. She is neither old nor young, but mature enough to have had some experience of life's com-plexities. She appreciates antiquities even when she's not sophisticated about them, and she enjoys learning more. It's a plus to develop stories that contain new information about interesting areas the reader doesn't already know a great deal about. Make sure the information is not presented in a didactic way, but as a method of fleshing out and advancing the story. There is an erotic element in the book that occasionally raises her eyebrows without offending her personal taste. Her need to get inside people's heads is bolstered by the fact that the characters are neither black nor white, but inhabit a world filled with shades of gray, resembling in many ways the one she has lived in all her life, yet different enough to awaken and compel her interest.

These are the elements of engagement. Even though I am a man, my female target reader resembles me in terms of many of my interests, because I don't care for cardboard characters either. My murderer is more likely to be your neighbor who simply got into an unmanageable situation and made a series of wrong choices, than he is to be a chain-saw killer lurking in your back yard whose motives can never be understood beyond brainless, drooling malice. For me, this makes the plot possibilities more interesting, the identifications more challenging, and the solutions occasionally more tragic.

Finally, there is humor. I can't go to the grocery store without an occasional chuckle, and living in México provides me with an endless series of ironic jokes. Many of them are about my constant attempts to understand my adopted culture. I can't write so much as a page without some of this humor slipping in. My target reader also enjoys a spontaneous laugh, and she soon recognizes that in my books she is connected to someone who cannot take himself seriously all the time. This makes my writing more accessible, and it provides relief from the serious parts. This benefit of not sustaining anything at the same tone for a prolonged period is one we'll revisit in a later chapter.

So there she is. As I work on the twelfth of these mysteries, I see her better than ever. Of course, I no longer have to ask myself who she is, as I did in the beginning, because by now I know her well. With this information I can focus on my goal for my book, which is always the same in fiction—to move her, to provide for her an emotional experience unlike those she normally has in her life. If sometimes in the morning when I boot the laptop after breakfast, she is there with a charming fan letter, I know

I've succeeded. I answer each one—never a weighty task—and her final question is often this: when is the next Paul Zacher mystery coming?

Fine, you say with a slight degree of impatience. Although you once spent five days in Cancun and were sick for the last three of them, you have never lived in México, or even farther than a mile from where you grew up in Lincoln, Nebraska. You've held a job with the same insurance company since you dropped out of college in your junior year. You never married, although you once turned down a tempting offer from a man who, at eight years your senior, you thought was a little too old for you. Down the road you could imagine the liver spots on his hands, even though he was only thirty-six at that time. The range of your experience, in fact, other than a two-month affair with a coworker that left you more embarrassed than fulfilled, is not much broader than your thumb. You wouldn't recognize a Mayan ceramic piece if you knocked it off the table during a quick lunch at Arby's. You know only too well that you're overly conservative in your life, even though you've always voted Democratic. For you habit tends to be stronger than inspiration, yet you secretly harbor a fervid desire to write that is increasingly shredding your peace of mind, even as you cultivate

a bland and unthreatening façade so as not to alarm
your friends and coworkers. There are even times
when you feel the answer might be science fiction—
this from a person who sometimes can't manage her
hair drier. Lord! And you thought life was supposed
to get easier.

Well, why not start with this? Your target
reader for the book you can't bring yourself to start
looks something like you, the imaginary reader of this
book that I've sketched above in such detail. She's followed the rules all her life, too, and she's sick of it.
Now she's ready for a blowout. Like most of us in
uninspiring positions, she has internalized her frus-
trations for years, yet she knows nothing about guns
and is not about to go postal. In fact, seeing them
as similar victims, she bears no real malice toward
anyone around her. But if she could blow the system sky high in a way that would make everyone in
her mindless situation, men or women, stand up and
cheer, she would bloody well do it. And then sleep
better because of it. Yes, this is still your story, but is
there anyone else out there who can connect to it? If
you have gotten this far, you now know they're not
only out there, they're waiting for your book.

The pathway into writing your new book
is provided by the contents of your own heart and

mind. Only you can read them, and only if you have the nerve. If you suspect that most people don't, you are correct. You know your family couldn't. These elements can be prickly and uncomfortable. They can torture you in the small hours of the morning, and you cannot talk about them to your friends because they might be too shocking. Yet, how you got to this point demands explanation, at least to yourself. How did it all begin? What decisions did you make at sixteen or even twelve that now maintain your life clicking along between the rails of a narrow course you don't remember consciously choosing? You see instantly what a task this could be, merely to get at the truth, to dig it out and tell it well. It need not be an autobiography or a memoire, but your emotions and experiences could still brilliantly animate the actors as you moved them across your stage. Why, it would be more than passionate, it would absorb your current and future life! You could be—if only you could pull it off—a writer!

So it's clear now that the target reader is a person who looks somewhat like you. Most writers write first for themselves anyway, creating books they would like to read but can't always find, so writing for this target reader's taste and interests will not in itself be a stretch. The largest part of it is to understand who she is in order to know what she's looking for as you begin to place those first lines on the page.

In a burst of optimism, at the top margin you have already entered the two words that suddenly read like a sentence of death: Chapter One. You instinctively shift your eyes elsewhere, but the rest of the page yawns blankly, which is even more disconcerting.

What follows is more challenging to writers both experienced and inexperienced than almost every other aspect of the craft. The first few words are critical in making an impression on the reader, and at the same time they seem to commit the writer to an established direction he may not be ready to take. In itself the prospect of starting a book can seem enormously daunting. The outcome is often that the writer sits looking at the blank page for an hour and then walks away without having composed a single word.

One remedy is to begin in a different place in the story, perhaps with a pair of characters in a conversation you know is coming up later in the book. Any part after the opening words will be less fraught with anxiety. For some writers, this may not be appealing because they need to think of the book more sequentially. They will do better starting at the beginning, because without that as an anchor, it can seem like stumbling around in a swamp with no firm footing.

Another approach is easing into the project through exercises. Here is one that often works to limber up. It will help get your head in shape for what's coming.

Exercise One

Every day for thirty days write a two-paragraph description of a different character, each time based on a real person you know. Don't skip a day. The goal is to have these characters recognizable—without being named—to someone who also knows them. All of these pieces should have a sense of completeness, as small as they are. The opening and the final lines should read as such.

On a daily basis, the limited scale of this exercise is unthreatening, and it has the stealth property of having the writer develop a polished shorthand for character development within that two paragraph limit. I know a number of people who have gotten far more skillful at characterization over the thirty days by using this method. They found that after five or six the task got so much easier that they could relax and enjoy it, tracing each day the progress they made by comparing the current effort with the early ones.

Exercise Two

When this is complete, on each of the thirty days following, write a single page of dialog between one pair of those characters, working through the list, putting together unlikely combinations—which you will quickly discover makes for interesting conversations. Review the chapter below titled Dialog. Again, the task is small in scale and will feel unthreatening. Like the character sketches, each piece should be polished and have a clear beginning and a plausible end. After sixty days you will have far more command of your skills, less anxiety in confronting the novel's first blank page, and without realizing it, you will have developed the habit of *working every day*. You have been snookered into adding a productive habit to your repertoire. Another positive outcome is that you have, without feeling much stress, created sixty different opening lines. Not bad for someone accustomed to fleeing the sight of a blank page.

Now every day is a work day, when in the past you have gone for months without putting a single word to paper. It should become a habit you need not think about, like brushing your teeth. We don't want to force ourselves to write, nor do we want to feel guilty if we're not writing. We write merely because it's what we do. It requires no special thought, because when we're in it, it is much like the Zone in sports—it's automatic and unforced. This daily engagement has the further value of guiding your story past the foreground of your thinking, and enrolling the vast unbridled resources of your unconscious as a participant. You should soon be dreaming about your characters. Often they will surprise you by what they say and do, as if they don't always need to consult you. This is good. Some writers keep a notepad by their pillow. In the morning, filter through these nocturnal sessions carefully; much of this material will be useless, but often you'll discover a prize.

Having done both the character and dialog exercises, the developing writer will bring to his project a ready set of tools he can use all the time. This is a confidence builder. He knows he can get at least some of it right, even at the beginning. By now he also realizes that it's not so difficult to improve a line later, which brings up the topic of revision, one we'll get to in a later chapter.

How long should you expect the writing of your book to take? There is no set answer to this, but I cringe when I meet someone who's been working on a book for eight or ten years. I can understand that any writer might have a limit to the time he can spend on a manuscript, but the danger in having it run too long is that the process becomes stretched too thin. You loose the ferment of your unconscious mind, the interaction between different thought levels, and the working process of your dreams. The more time that elapses between work sessions, the more your story is sidelined by your brain. You don't want to have to start shoveling to get at it. Hit the ground running. If you can write your book inside a year, all the better.

I had a conversation with a woman one evening who was thinking she wanted to try writing some stories. I asked what was holding her back, since she was in a position of soon being retired, and time would not be an issue. She was afraid, she said, that her stories might have been told before.

I replied that most likely they had been, in one form or another. Some writing coaches believe that fewer than a dozen different plots exist, and each new story is a rehash of one of them. The real question is what the writer brings to these well-used story lines from her own experience, what detail she uses to flesh them out, and what characters she invents to carry her message. Your stories will be unique, even when the plot is not, I told her, because you develop them from your own psyche and life experience. The plot you may be sharing with another writer is only the roadmap you will fill with your own blend of animation and detail. This is true of every author.

Reservations like the one she expressed are a variety of block, which is a self-imposed limitation, often a kind of paralysis like the page one jitters we talked about above. Here is a statement of critical importance that I make to everyone who says to me they are suffering from writer's block—a subject I know something about. It is not about *you*, my friend, not at all. It is only about the material you wish to write, and the approach you bring to it. It is all about process, never about personality. Get used to the fact that your ego is no more important than a fly on the wall of your own creativity. Never fear failure—it's only a poor choice of words to describe one of a series of steps on the way to success, not all of which are of equal value. But they all must be taken, and something can be learned from every one of them.

4.

BEAUTIFUL WRITING

In the course of writing eighteen books, many questions have come to mind about how to make the process easier. Is there a theory or a formula that works? I'll get to those issues, but first, what about the words themselves? Are they the same words you use in your conversation on a daily basis? You are already aware that some situations, like talking on the phone, employ a verbal shorthand that differs from normal conversation. In your book, should you be colloquial, or try to sound literary? Do your written words come from a loftier and more eloquent collection in your mind, a special set you don't use every day? Don't you need a word resource like this to make your work stand out? After all, you consider yourself a serious writer, at least in your dreams. Shouldn't your writing possess a certain level of beauty or elegance? You've heard more than once that writing is an art.

Many writing coaches counsel their students that the consciously "beautiful writing" you create in fiction usually goes unnoticed by the public. Their readers are too busy marching through the narrative on their way to see what happens next. After all, they argue, with good reason, as writers, isn't our primary job to be storytellers first and prose stylists later? What does it matter how it's done, as long as it's clear, concise, and well-paced. Aren't most bestselling authors merely good pacers? Surely, we've all noticed that not many of them are good at writing.

If you're like most writers, however, you still have that nagging need to take wing now and then, to show the world—and yourself—what you're capable of when you're at your best. Your gut feeling is that this needs to be more than merely the same bland colloquial English you use at the supermarket. You know you can be more literary, and you've already got a long list of vivid but rarely seen words you haven't been able to find a place for recently waiting for the right paragraph.

Once you've placed them on the page, however, these minor operatic arias act like a Mafia informant—they tend to take on a certain kind of immunity. No matter how much they might need pruning or even complete elimination, they linger under your loving eyes like a wayward favorite child you cannot bring yourself to discipline. No matter that they lack context, looking as out of place as a gold nugget lying on a muddy riverbank.

Some successful writers have converted this pitfall into a virtue. One of these is Cormac McCarthy. He appears to be a tweedy gentleman well into his seventies. He has won numerous honors, including the National Book Award, so his process deserves a closer look. He takes a long time to craft a book and displays great pride in his style, which tends to shed both punctuation and dialog attributions. When I read his work, I envision a much younger man as the author, wearing a gritty headband that still does not prevent the sweat from dripping into his eyes. His arms are well muscled and his knuckles scarred from intimate contact with his craft. His face is shadowed by dirt or coal dust. He has taken care to hammer each word into place, and then pulled it out again with a pair of tongs and re-hammered it. His prose often aches on the page. It is full of bold examples of beautiful writing; they are angular and knobby, faceted and dense with meaning. When they work, which is most of the time, they feel brilliant, if never entirely natural. They demand attention for themselves, and indirectly, for the author's prowess. When they don't work, they fall into a black hole devoid of meaning, and they invite the reader to think about all the other examples he had used that stood out like a concrete block in the road. Whether they succeed or not you are always aware of Cormac McCarthy as the skilled laboring man at your side, sweating and straining at his craft.

This problem reminds me of a dinner party where every element was planned long in advance and emerges perfectly: the décor, the food, the wine, and the company selected for their established chemistry. Visible through the kitchen door, the host and hostess are working themselves to death for your assured enjoyment. You are impressed and flattered as you relish the wine from an obscure vineyard in Burgundy that's been in the same family since the tenth century. Yet, feeling that you ought to rise and cheer each new triumph, you are not having any fun.

One rule of hospitality is this: never let them see you sweat. As authors, each of us is the reader's host, and the same rule applies to all of us.

Another author who has mastered beautiful writing is John Updike, who died a few years ago. I recently reread his four Rabbit novels, written at ten-year intervals. His method is to burnish rather than bludgeon, and his prose his honed and polished to a gemlike luster. It is the style of a penetrating mind. You sense he would prefer not to use any word that had ever been used before, at least in the way he's planning to use it. When successful, the effect can be more than illuminating; it can be stunning. When it fails, it leaves the reader with her mouth open, wondering what on earth Updike was trying to say.

Make no mistake; skilled writing involves taking real risks. This chapter is not a caution against taking them, but a guide on how to take them for the greatest effect, which means invisibly. Writing is not for people of great modesty, or for cowards, since it involves launching yourself through the air without a net, knowing that you will occasionally fall and bruise your own self-respect. This often-painful process is the way your skills advance. It is no surprise therefore, that even Cormac McCarthy and John Updike sometimes fail, but an occasional failure does not diminish their long record of success, nor will it yours, even if it's much shorter and more tentative. The bottom line is this: Take the risk, and if it does not result in a triumph every time, don't hesitate to cut it. Over the long haul it will be well worth the chances you took. Each time you extend yourself in this way, make sure to read the passage aloud or have someone else read it to you. The spoken word will expose awkwardness or an outright blunder more easily than the written.

What I find lacking in both McCarthy and Updike is the *appearance* of not working very hard to make their magical effects happen, the sense of having tossed off that brilliant paragraph without a second thought, without kneading it, rolling it over, punching it down, and kneading it again. And then moving off to the next triumph, without looking back over their shoulders.

The word I use for this ease of delivery that I often find missing is grace. It is conveying the illusion of being casual and uncalculating in your craft, even as you lay down the brilliant phrase. Properly done, it is natural, masterful, and yet informal. It is magisterial yet intimate—a tall order. It is the flick of the wrist of a great painter as he lays down a brushstroke that is luminous and correct, but almost looks unplanned.

One writer who was a master of this was Somerset Maugham, who died at 91 in 1965. While he never appeared to work as hard as McCarthy or Updike at beautiful writing, it was often present in the precision of his prose. His work is layered with nuance, rather than crusty with meaning. His sentences often evoke rather than relate or explain. When they open a small, long-forgotten door in the reader's mind, emotions, thoughts and memories fly out in a rush, and they all combine to flesh out

Maugham's narrative. The following chapter contains more about this phenomenon.

Like Updike and McCarthy, Maugham himself is often present on the page. But rather than sweating and pretending he's invisible, he is usually to be found seated on the veranda of a house near Kuala Lumpur with a tall cool gin drink, or at a sidewalk café in Nice or Cap Ferrat. He is unafraid to be a character, major or minor, in his own fiction, yet his work is largely not autobiographical. His opening lines often spring from his own experience, but usually only as a starting point. For example, this first sentence from a short story called *Jane* is typical: "I remember very well the occasion on which I first saw Jane Fowler."

How simple that is, and how unaffected. This unselfconscious presence is what gives the story both its intimacy and its credibility—its grace. The reader almost feels she's in a conversation with Maugham, relaxed and personal. If she reached out and touched his hand, it would seem quite natural. There is never a false note, nor does it ever feel reworked, although I imagine Maugham must have done considerable revision, just as we all do. Yet the ease of it is never strained. This is a goal we can all adopt for our own work.

So the question remains: Beautiful writing—who needs it?

I think we all do. Certainly writers need to take wing now and then, to lift off and soar above the mundane, the ordinary grocery list kind of prose that gets us from point A to B in a story. But I believe the reader needs it too. When writing coaches discourage their students from attempting it, they perhaps fear its misuse more than they doubt its welcome by the reader when it's successfully done.

But of course, it's no different from successful entertaining: you must never let them see you sweat.

5.

THE READER'S ROLE

Now you are launched, and your book has progressed several pages past the opening sentence. You are trying to use the precise words you need and actively searching for "grace" as you do it, but without appearing to. It's not too soon to ask what role the reader plays in all of this. Is she merely passive, a page-turning sponge to absorb the author's efforts, or a mirror to reflect the glory of his prose? I'll try to illustrate the answer with this comparison.

Movies have been with us for about 115 years now. Their charm is obvious—movement, color, surround sound, and the impact of constantly changing visuals. Some even offer 3-D. Aren't they about the most stimulating entertainment possible? The violence especially is often more than you could ever imagine, or would want to. With all this, why would anyone bother to pick up a book anymore? After all, books are your grandmother's entertainment, and you can put as many greats before that *grand* as you want. They are *old stuff.* They are black and white; they are lines of print that only vary in length. Sitting on the shelf, you have to dust them periodically, and in humid climates, they often grow mold and develop strange odors. Furthermore, they're expensive. Only the airport racks furnish paperbacks that are about the same price as a movie ticket. Then there are the times when you have to go to your online dictionary to look up a word you don't know. Movies never make you work like that. You don't even have to think. In your busy life, that often feels like a plus.

When you look up at the screen, every square inch is filled. Nothing is left out, and no spaces are blank. You are shown only what the director decides you need to see, because the theater is darkened and nothing else is available to look at. What to feel and how to express it is illustrated for you, as the actors portray their scripted emotions. If you see a movie on television that you watched in the theater five years ago, that movie has not changed, although you have.

Here's the difference: the novel you are reading, if skillfully done, has *air* in it. The author has left invisible, yet elastic spaces for you to unconsciously insert your own reactions and experience, whether small or large. He does this by simply not telling you everything. He's holding back because he wants something from you—your participation. The very basic limitation of books, the way they are unable to show you everything in the story with all its detail, is also their principal strength. This inability of a book to offer visual elements, only to *stimulate* you visually, is a huge advantage, contrary to what you might think. As the reader, you are not only able, you are *required* to fill in the blanks, the *air*, to get maximum enjoyment from the book. Reading is a *participatory* experience in a way that movies can never be.

You, the reader, are at the writer's shoulder helping to create the book page by page. The writer has done his best to imply, suggest, stimulate, evoke, and hint, but every stroke of his pen is incomplete. It begs you to add actions and feelings you've experienced, the emotions you've felt, with all the subtleties that only your mind and history can bring. The author will etch on the page the smells, tastes, and colors that bloomed in his thoughts as he wrote, but you will insert your own twist and nuance to each of them, adding layers of connections to your own history, just as a painter's brushstroke is defined and articulated by the colors around it (*local color*). A good book is different to each of its readers, and that is part of why it works. Every good book is an entire repertory of human experience, as supplied by its crowd of readers.

Unlike in the movie, where you leave the theater with the ring of explosions still oppressing your ears, you finish reading a book with the awareness of having worked at it, a sense of fulfillment and achievement. A successful author will have lured you into contributing to this effort, and as a result, you are the coauthor, if not of the book itself, then of your *experience* of the book. You are in a relay race, and the writer has handed you the baton. It's your job now to take it home for the gold. Properly done, the book will leave you thinking that you're ready to go on another journey with this writer, because it's been rewarding in ways you hadn't anticipated. Where will he take you next time? It's as if you are already packed and ready to go.

And when you read that book once more, five years later, or ten, it will be a different book and a different journey, although the words on the page will not have changed, because you will bring to it the increased layers of your own experience and insights. Your collaboration with the author will be comprised of a different pair of people than it was the previous time, because you, the reader, have changed and evolved. More than any other reason, even great leather bindings with gold stampings, this is why we keep books on our shelves and in our lives.

This is why movies can never replace books.

So turn off your surround sound, your six-ty-inch flat screen, leave your car in the garage, and drop your 3-D glasses back into the drawer. Pick up a book and turn on your mind. No electricity is required because it's powered by magic, and you are the sorcerer.

The author must always be aware that writing needs to be interspersed with that air I mentioned, about what to leave out as much as what to put in. The problem is to find eloquence in the *unwritten* phrase, which is where the air lies. That sounds like getting something from nothing, which is not quite the case. The unwritten message will be supplied by the rhythm that led up to it, and by what the reader expects to find but does not. It will be about the mental process that follows when she realizes she has not been given what she expected on the page. She flips back to the previous one—did she skip over something? In other words, the absent phrase will acquire meaning through its context, rather than its presence.

Nothing is more frightening than the un-known, not even bad news. We can begin to adjust and process both good news and bad once we know it, but the unknown offers us nothing to work on.

In the absence of information, we manufacture our own fear, which can easily run ahead of reality.

Think of it this way. Imagine your character pushing open a squeaking door in a house she fears is haunted. As she leans into the darkened room, she whispers, "Bill? Are you in there?" The silence that follows when Bill fails to answer becomes saturated with fear, and the chapter ends with those words. She sees nothing, but what unseen figure might be watching her? The writer has no need to describe the character's reaction because the reader will supply every nuance of it herself as her blood suddenly runs cold. In fact, to have added even one more word would diminish the effect. As it is, what every reader adds herself will tend to be far more effective than what the writer could have supplied, because it will be what she felt at the most uniquely frightening moment of her life. Leaving the air for this will elicit the desired response from every reader.

In the passages above, where I wrote about Somerset Maugham being an evocative writer, opening a door in the mind to allow the escape of recollection, memory and emotion, I could also have mentioned this stimulating silence, because properly handled, the absence of words on the page can be equally evocative, and sometimes more so. The ability to pull this off is called knowing when to quit, and restraint is not the easiest of skills to master. We are usually inclined to think in terms of what we should be adding to the story, rather than what we should be omitting.

The beginning writer, in particular, often worries that he has not explained things nearly enough, and in going overboard, limits the reader's vital input.

6.

CHARACTERS

It is appropriate to now examine the people who will populate your fictional world. Later we'll talk about where they come from, and about location and setting, the landscape they inhabit. We will discuss plot, dialog, and point of view. But first, let's bring the characters onstage and have a look at them. This sequence makes sense because it is more natural to shape a plot to a character, and a location to a plot and character, than the reverse. Once your actors are up, walking around and speaking, they will tend to start acting more and more on their own. Often they already know what they want. You will still be in control to some degree, but it is wise not to disregard what they come up with, because if you have constructed them well, they may sometimes disregard you.

The plot will be somewhat contingent on these people, so it is better not to think of it as the first piece of business in planning your story. You may outline the sequence of the action, but you will find going forward that the characters will tend to take things into their own hands. Do not fight this. Well-crafted characters often know what they are going to do better than you do.

The people we see before us will not be named the Antagonist, the Protagonist, or the Second Ingénue, although you will see these terms in formulaic pieces on how to write. Just as we have not made reference to formulas earlier, we will not use them now for one simple reason: there is no formula that will tell you how to write well. If there was, it would be like following a recipe, and anyone could do it. Great writers would flow in unstoppable torrents from creative writing programs all over the country. A random glance at the stream of books coming both from New York and from self-published authors will tell you this is not happening.

Your characters have real names because they are real people that you have given birth to in your mind. Don't think that diminishes their reality. If you regard them as first dowager, the garbage man, or the vampire's consort, that is as close as you will ever get to them, and it will never be close enough to bring them alive for you. Your readers will react in the same way. Discard these stereotypes—they will neither engage the reader's interest in the opening chapter nor sustain yours over the length of a book. You will need to be on a first name basis with all of them, even the ones who make you uncomfortable—perhaps those especially. It's all right for your work to have an edgy quality.

Nor will your characters be the richest, the most beautiful, the sexiest, or the smartest people that ever lived, privately jetting off to Cannes or Rio at the drop of a party invitation. Ho hum. Yet, don't readers want escape from their drab, routine lives? Of course they do, but when they pick up a book that is done in imitation of the above formula, they will find it exactly like ten million other books built on the same set of stereotypes, so it provides no escape. It offers only more of the same drab, brain-dead routine they're trying to flee. They already know from reenacting the formula of going to work every day, day after day, that liberation does not await them in *more* formulas. Demonstrating this with your book will not cause them to rush forward and friend you on Facebook.

Beware of bringing your actors onstage too quickly. The reader needs time to memorize their names and associate a few key characteristics with each of them. Bring them in one or two at a time

and have them interact a bit before introducing any
more.

Often your actors can be clustered in groups.
If I look at my mysteries I discover a trio of core
characters: the 35-year-old painter/detective, his 28-
year old historian girlfriend, and the 58-year-old retired homicide detective. It may look like a formula,
but it is saved from being that by its necessary base
in the way they function with each other. The ex-
cop brings experience and knowledge of procedure,
the painter brings visual insight, and the historian,
being a Méxican woman, brings a contrasting cultural and gender perspective. None of them are super
heroes or extreme experts in their field. In addition
to these roles, they all bring their strong individual
point of view, and each of them can play against type
now and then. We all entertain some contradictory
elements in our own character, and so do they.
If your core characters are not fundamentally in
conflict with each other, which is the case with these
three, who are usually aimed at the same goal—to
trap the villains—then it helps to make them sufficiently different from each other to establish a natural ongoing contrast in their attitudes and approach
to crime-solving. Their conversations will reflect their
differing strategies and assumptions, which keeps

them lively. They will have occasional deeper misunderstandings and disagreements. It is the character of their interaction that drives these stories, and each of them is featured in the lead at various times. When you begin to draw your characters, give their coming interaction considerable thought. It will be the source of drama, as well as both information and emotional engagement for your reader. While liking all of them, she will identify with the one she feels closest to.

Notice now the *individual* appearance of your actors' faces. They bear the stamp of their life stories. Think of how well they are named, because some names will fit and some will not. I recently saw a promotion where a writer was offering to sell off the opportunity to name his characters for a monetary contribution to his self-publication costs. Indeed, I thought. This is a good way to end up with a detective character named Dipsy Doodle. Names are far more important than that. I shudder when I imagine an 86-year-old woman named Candy. Don't give your character a frivolous name unless she has a frivolous job to do in your story. This does not mean the names must mimic the job. Don't name your character Edsel if he's a Ford dealer, or Steve Adore if he unloads cargo ships. Then there's your hero with old-fashioned values, Vic Taurian.

Not every character will receive a name. Actors performing minor functions, those who will be killed off quickly, others that have no major place in the principal action, can remain nameless. In the early pages, the reader makes an effort to assign names to characters and remember them. Don't tax this propensity of hers, it's an important way of maintaining her connection to the story. Readers always remain closer to people they know by name.

One writer I know has the habit of drawing his villains as the most vile people who ever lived. They never have a single redeeming characteristic. I have tactfully suggested to him that they're devoid of interest because of this. Because their personalities lack complexity, they display no *tension* on the page. Since they avidly embrace evil nonstop, they are never in conflict with themselves. They are no more vivid or compelling than inverted saints.

"But," he has sometimes replied, "how else can you tell they're the villains?"

Maybe a nametag would help, but I thought we had stopped using these terms. No villain, no saint, and no kindly grandmother will take the stage in our stories. There is only the conflict among shades of gray (but not average) kinds of people trying to get from here to there, and the problems resulting from their desires. They all have names and personalities. Some will leave a body or two behind them on the trail, ineffectively covered over with brush to try to conceal it. Others will work for positive goals, and in the process, paper over their own spooky tendencies with good deeds and be regarded as heroes, another term we'll walk away from without regret.

To have the character drawn in shades of utter black is also to disrespect your reader. She is able to tell on her own, by her personal experience, when a guy has ethical and moral problems. She's seen them every day at the water cooler. And if the demon is shown so far away from the gray on gray world she inhabits, she will not connect with your other characters either because she has not connected with *you*. Remember, this reader is working at your side to help create the story by filling the airy spots with her own input. To do this, she must find herself in sympathy with what you're doing. A solidly vicious one-dimensional character provides no air spaces to fill.

If she does not connect in this way, she will not invest herself in your book, and when her friend asks her what she thought, she will respond with this, "I stayed with it to the end, but you know, I'm not sure why. I really didn't buy the story." Nor will her friend. Word-of-mouth promotion is important, and you need to earn it.

What we want are characters that are relatable. The reader should find points of connection with your killer no less than with the others. You don't need to tell her that murder is wrong. You're not running a Sunday school. Show her the character in action and allow her to make her own judgments. Here is the idea of respecting the reader again, and you will see it often—don't tell her what to think, even when you suspect she is not always going to think the way you do. Allow her to find the bad guy rather attractive, if that can serve your purpose, and sometimes it does. Allow her to think about other choices that your characters might have made, but did not. Be sure to leave those air spaces throughout the story, and especially in moments of high tension, so she can insert her own feelings and insights by recalling and reliving similar moments in her own life.

One of the great benefits of using complex villains is that you can explore the ways they mask or rationalize their actions, both to deceive themselves and the people around them. For me, this is one of the most interesting parts of a story, and one that is not possible to develop if the villain is one-dimensional.

In terms of playing against type, which is what uniting the bad and the good in unexpected combinations to form shades of gray is called, the late Patricia Highsmith was a master. *The Talented Mr. Ripley* is the first of five serial mysteries with the same principal character. Ripley is a conman, identity thief, and a murderer, as well as a proficient amateur painter and a student of the harpsichord. Masquerading as a man he murdered introduces endless plot possibilities. I enjoy the way this plays, and Highsmith has pulled off the nearly impossible feat of making us like, identify, and even root for a killer. How is it possible that we always want him to triumph over the decent people around him? His character is not all black, and he shares many attributes of normal people, their drives and ambitions. Ripley possesses a level of refinement that is not a pretense. Later on, he's married to a charming French woman who has no idea of his past, and we still admire him as he deceives her about his present activities, even another necessary murder where he hides the body in their wine cellar.

Through the masterful wiles of Highsmith, we have become co-conspirators in his crimes, possibly the highest form of reader participation. We have

followed a character across our own moral boundaries, and we still support him. No writing formula
could ever lead us to do this. Doesn't it suggest that
we have found within ourselves the same need Ripley
has to survive no matter what he's done? Isn't that
the point of relatability? How could that be unless
we all contain elements of his character within our
own minds? I'll examine this in more detail in the
next chapter, Getting Inside Yourself, where you will
discover how to find the talented Mr. Ripley within
each of us.

I have thought a great deal about how
Patricia Highsmith pulled this off, not that we want to
imitate her or anyone, but it raises key issues about
that idea of the relatability of a character. This is a
prime feature of successful fiction. When it works,
and you see Bill come onto the page, you don't say,
here's the third villain's assistant, you say, "My god, I
wish I had the guts to do what Bill just did. And I'm
glad he did it."

In Ripley's case I think it works because it's
all handled in the context of normalcy. It's as if she
wrote, *Ripley bought six ripe grapefruit, stopped for flowers,*
opened a checking account, and killed the cop standing in his
driveway as he drove up and parked beside the kitchen door.
The key is handling all of these events in the same

tone, as if none were unexpected. His actions take on the quality of what any of us would do in his place, and one flows from another. There is a great sense of contingency in Highsmith's fiction. All actions have consequences, which is something to bear in mind when you are working out a plot. We are persuaded to suspend our disbelief, even as we nod, saying, good job, getting rid of that body in the canal so quickly. It doesn't look any different from normal behavior.

This approach reminds me of *The Godfather*, where the multiple killings occur mainly for business reasons. We have no problem sympathizing with the murderous Corleone clan in their struggle with rival groups. Part of it is that they remain "principled." Their resistance to the onset of drug distribution by other Mafia families, preferring to stay with gambling, loan sharking, and prostitution, allows us to see them as touchingly old fashioned. We are able to interpret this as a virtue, and their restraint helps us to define their competition as evil. Aren't we also almost virtuous when we embrace the lesser of two evils as our choice? We can almost argue that we do it from principle, once we've declined to take the darker path. The traditional vices are good enough for us, thank you.

I don't raise these quirky but still impressive

triumphs of Patricia Highsmith and Mario Puzo as examples for writers starting out, since they require a delicate balancing act that draws on the most developed skills. But they do illustrate what is possible when the writer ignores the lure of formulas and thinks strictly in terms of individual actors and situations. For the reader to find a character sympathetic is not always contingent on his level of personal virtue. Often that has nothing to do with it.

Good guys can be more difficult to write of convincingly than bad guys. One reason is that they're often not as goal oriented, or when they are, the goal may not be as worthy of obstruction; like finishing the new orphanage on time, no matter what. Here is an area where the writer wants to be sure his good character is as flawed as any of us. The conflict between his benign instincts and his questionable urges or downright weaknesses can be the basis of drama, but if we are shown only his saintly luster we are likely to nod off. I like to detect in every major character the seeds of both disaster and victory, suspended in some degree of tension. I want to see the mother superior of the convent watching male pornography on her laptop in the wee hours. We need to be in suspense about which will eventually triumph, since drama requires the presence of considerable doubt at times.

I believe that in life we know people by the way they act, rather than what they say they believe. I'll modify that for fiction. Show us your character in motion, doing things that demonstrate his nature, rather than telling us passively what he is like, although combining that with some direct description is often most effective as part of the package. Here's an example from the second of my mysteries, *The Fifth Codex*:

Professor Sandoval was a big barrel-chested man with iron gray hair. He wore a blue blazer with gray slacks and a white shirt open at the neck. His expensive-looking frameless glasses were the kind where the bows attach directly to the lenses. He appeared to have just shaved; even the jowls flanking his chin were perfect, however, the curly hairs in his eyebrows seemed bent on escape. I guessed he was in his late fifties, like Cody. His walk was a little odd, with one leg never quite catching up to the other as he moved. He noticed me observing his gait.

"Snakebite," he said as he approached. "Got it on an old dig at Tikal in Guatemala. The nerves in my leg never healed right."

Beyond that, we don't have to announce that he's an archaeologist working in Latin America, and probably an expert on Mayan civilization. Look for painless ways like this to deliver background information. They do not slow the narrative. We also realize that Sandoval feels the need to explain his only physical shortcoming, a hint that he may be vain and egotistical. None of this will prevent him from being a likeable, if somewhat flawed, character as the story unfolds.

In an earlier scene in the same book, painter/detective Paul Zacher is meeting a new model, Lynn Washburn, one he hasn't worked with before. As an artist, he's fascinated by her nearly anorexic appearance. Lacking a robe, she has changed into a nightgown behind a screen before she comes back to the platform where she'll pose. Paul watched her emerge.

"I'm ready."
"Should I take this off?"
"If you're ready. The seat should be warm now." She stood up and pulled the nightgown up as far as mid thigh and then stopped.
"I've never done this before." Her small

voice came from inside the nightgown.

"I've done it hundreds of times. Don't be nervous. Think of your body as landscape. I do."

I heard a deep breath from the nightgown, and then she pulled it off the rest of the way. She was like an anatomy lesson; I could see all of her bones. As she sat down on the chair again her hips moved visibly in their sockets. Her breasts were small and pointed, and I knew they would stay exactly the same way when she leaned forward on her elbows. Her nipples swelled slightly and were not fully defined. Immediately I saw a new set of possibilities; the sheer angularity of her body would resolve into planes and hollows in a way unlike any model I'd ever painted.

In many of her appearances, Lynn's gaunt physical character is her most prominent feature. It becomes a metaphor for her tentative approach to life.

Don't overlook that potential of clothing, or its absence, and accessories to suggest aspects of your character. Here is a paragraph from the eleventh Zacher mystery, as yet untitled and unfinished:

When the man came in his look immediately reminded me of his father. He had the same big chest over a narrow waist, and wavy dark hair with a widow's peak. His once crisp tropical shirt, now damp and wilted, was open two buttons to underline his virility, and his tight jeans said he might still be in play as he bent over and stood his rolled up umbrella in the corner near the door. Water streamed off it into the spreading puddle. He wore an elaborately worked Navajo concho belt in silver and turquoise. It would have taken a skilled craftsman a week to make his stamped and embroidered Western boots, now soaked. I put his age at about thirty-five.

Even before he speaks, the way this character presents himself tells a great deal about his pretensions. It's also a chance to plant elements that will be significant later, because when he is murdered shortly after this scene, the concho belt is stolen. It will turn up late in the book in the scene that reveals who killed him. We'll talk about foreshadowing of this kind in the plot chapter.

These descriptive elements can also be

contradictory, as in the following scene from the twelfth Paul Zacher Mystery, unfinished but titled, Veracruz. Paul, Maya, and Cody of the Zacher Agency are in the San Miguel Morgue with Inspector Delgado of the San Miguel Judicial Police. He lifts a dead girl's hand from beneath the sheet for them to examine:

"Nice job," Maya said, immediately examining the manicure. It was a four-color design in an Art Deco style. I glanced down at the toes, and in this better working light I now saw a simpler version of the same theme. Delgado turned the hand over. The palm and fingers were calloused and rough. Cody studied the wrist and forearm.

An expensive manicure on a body with rough and calloused palms? This girl speaks to them even in death.

What if you are having trouble getting inside the head of one of your characters? You can see him, but you can't make the leap to getting him to open his mouth, and when he moves about, he's listless and lacks distinguishing attributes.

One solution to this was the habit Somerset Maugham had of carrying a notebook with him. When he found himself looking at people with interesting physical traits, or with distinctive body language and gestures, he wrote them up. Over time, he had a behavioral reference library of such notes that he could call upon to bring a character to life. You can draw on your own collection of quirks and gestures while still developing the essence of the character from your own psyche.

If you did not do the exercise with a series of two paragraph character descriptions I talked about in Getting Started, you might now take a look at that too. Even use it with three or four of your main characters. Another option is this one:

Exercise Three

Write a paragraph of dialog for one of your principal actors. Give it the appropriate body language and facial mannerisms. Keep the content of it slightly ambiguous, but in character. Now put that identical paragraph in the mouth of one of your other characters, one you are having trouble with. Change the body language and gestural style to give it a slightly different meaning—one that fits that character. You can repeat this across the slate of your entire character group, ranging across gender lines.

A final note: I can name some major authors who look down on their characters, as if they were superior to them. This testifies to the author's need for status more than anything else. Personally, I wouldn't waste time on a character I regarded with contempt. As writers it is our job to embrace and love the characters we have made, even the weak ones and the villains. Wayward and wicked though they may be, they are still our children. Being judgmental is a task for the reader, never for the writer.

7.

GETTING INSIDE YOURSELF

Here is a phrase I've put on the back cover of a number of my books at the bottom of the author bio. "While the author has acknowledged being no single one of his characters, he also admits to being all of them."

All of them? If you've read any of my mysteries, that statement raises your eyebrows, because my characters are often complex and diverse.

I typically don't base them on real people; which I find too limiting, and I want characters to inhabit my books who will get up and walk around on their own, without reference to what a living version of them might say or do. This is not to say I won't borrow a trait or two now and then, or a bit of background. For example, to my vampire, Monty Townshend, in *And Dark My Desire*, I gave a history as a dance host on the *SS Ile de France* in the early thirties. A friend of mine was a dance host for years on cruise ships worldwide, and I thought that would be a splendid role for a vampire, a great way to meet people he might want to get to know a little more intimately, mostly single women and widows. You see, Monty had developed a taste for blood from the femoral artery, located in the groin.

In a broader sense, all my fictional characters come from within my own mind. Since we are not likely to ever see anyone as they see themselves, why not abandon the reality around us as an approach to character development and dig deeper inside our own psyche? You can still use any quirky and telling visual traits you've observed in real people, but characters are like plants in topiary; you can train and shape them to your needs.

One potential obstacle to this approach is that generating characters internally requires making some uncomfortable assumptions about ourselves. Yet we know the other components of any novel come from inside our heads, so why not the characters? If you can write about Timbuktu by doing a little online research, you also can write about someone you've never met or previously imagined by probing deeper into the Internet of your own mind. Yes, it requires imagination, but you have been imagining yourself as a successful writer all along, right? You must have the knack.

But, you say, squirming in your seat, what about those truly *evil* people, the killers? I'm a decent human being. I've raised a family. Soon I'll be a grandparent and a babysitter. So how can I write my way inside the head of a killer?

I can acknowledge all that and still believe you will find the killers within yourself too. They are not all depraved lunatics, which, as I suggested above, make boring characters because they're so one-dimensional. As a mystery writer, I thoroughly enjoy developing killers whose psychology is a mixed bag, which is true of most of us. Many of them are like me in their tastes and attitudes. Often they're sophisticated people, appreciating fine wine and well-written books. They like to travel, and they possess an educated eye for paintings. Where I depart from these killers that inhabit my head is that I get my revenge on the page, so I have never needed to act out fantasies of this kind. But have I fantasized about murdering my crooked business partner or my idiotic neighbor whose dog was ruining my property values? Of course, and I know exactly where I would shoot them first. I can place this image into the mind of my murderer in a heartbeat. Now, the difference between my fictional murderer and me is mainly one of opportunity and the intensity of my needs. My principal need is to stay out of jail and write books on the shady second floor terrace of my house in México, just what I am doing at this moment.

The principal difference between people or characters we think of as good or as bad is this: how far is any one of them prepared to go in acting out desires we all have? We are not different in kind from them, only in degree of need, emphasis, and desperation. Don't we also make stupid mistakes at times?

Look at some of the varieties of human behavior. We have all known horrendous people, just as we've all known those who've surprised us by their unexpected kindness. We've observed every degree of difference between. In my view, the potential for all kinds of behavior exists in every one of us. I can be both Mother Teresa and Josef Stalin, (both came from a religious background), just as I am both George Washington and Richard Nixon. I am your ninety-two-year-old neighbor who doesn't know what day it is, and I am also the baby on your lap who doesn't either. We all share the same pool of possibility. As the author, that pool is your playing field, your ball court, and your chessboard. Your task is to feel comfortable ranging over it, learning its rules and potential, and exploiting its resources.

As you do this, never be afraid to play against

type, that mixture of grays I mentioned above. If you write about an accountant, your reader will have conventional expectations that you can violate to surprise her. When you do this, make sure you do it with good reason and with some foreshadowing, not merely on whim. If the accountant is a weekend rock climber, mention the equipment on his garage wall when he gets out of his car, or notice the scars on his knees one day when you see him in shorts at the company softball game.

Pay attention in detail to the mannerisms and conversational style of the opposite sex. You will need to write convincingly as both men and women. Listen to what they say and how they say it. What assumptions do women make when they talk to men, and vice versa? Conversation contains different levels of information, some of it accurate on the face of it, but often statements are designed to tell you what to think, rather than what the speaker thinks. Recognize the difference and use it.

This is not a religious statement, nor is it New Age or mystical, but I am everybody and so are you. We both encompass all the human inclinations, and what makes us the unique individuals we are is the mix of those qualities that predominates. The law that forbids murder applies to all of us for good reason, not just to those who have a "tendency" to do it because of a deficient economic background, faulty parenting, or mental issues. That tendency is no more than a mathematical bias that causes one factor to become dominant over another in our behavior. The strange and startling ideas that you sometimes get are also lurking in the minds of others, many others, even though you think it's only you who harbors them on a bad day. Now that you know this, look around you, and look again over your shoulder. Some of those shadowy people back there under the trees are also writers, and the undetected complex monster in them equally inhabits you, gentle reader. I might have said this earlier, but this is as good a place as any: strong writers are people who have nothing more to lose because they have placed everything on the line. They have embraced the great range of their humanity, even where it slides into darkness. Ask Stephen King where he finds his material and his actors. He'll tell you he doesn't even have to leave the house or turn on his computer.

I can imagine that some of this is more than you wanted to know. Yet, this idea offers us an opportunity. We can, to use someone else's phrase, dare to be different. In this case, being different is merely admitting that we would like to have access to the darker and more difficult areas of our own minds—the ones that need a password.

Turning away, most people decline to learn what that password is. Writers don't have that option. The trick is to give ourselves permission to have our psyche made up partly of risky elements. But if we as writers persevere, once inside, that world locks much like the world we live in on a day-to-day basis, if somewhat darker in the shadows and rougher in texture. The difference is that once inside we know what we're looking at and we are free to use it. The password has merely opened the connection and our eyes. It's a new and larger bag of tricks. There is no need to conform to anyone's expectations as you draw the characters in your book. By looking into your own mind you have glimpsed the secrets of their hearts.

Because you are now the creator, you have entered the character zone, where anything is possible, all options are open. Haven't we all been just one or two mistakes away from committing a crime, or taking some action among our family or friends that was irreversible? Actions are available here that need not have been done before by someone else you know, or by you yourself, or anyone ever, if you can stretch that far. The only limiting factor is you and your ability to let yourself go. The characters you discover here are free to act on their own impulses, and are not beholden to anyone in the real world. This is a strength, not a limitation. It is where great characters are found, because the reader will recognize them from their occasional appearance in her own thoughts. They may act and look slightly different, but she will know them nonetheless, and she will be amazed at your insight, wondering how you managed to read the most private secrets of *her* mind. Part of this response will come from her filling the air in your story with parts of her own experience.

8.

PLOT

You will find practically as many definitions of plot as there are plots, even if there are only twelve. You will discover graphs of peaks and valleys, bell curves, and a dozen other serpentine profiles. People have theorized endlessly about what a plot is. I will offer a definition that is not profound, since profundity is not needed here, but it is functional: the plot is the roadmap of your story. I like the graphic element in describing it as a landscape.

I have said this before, and it bears repeating. As writers we are storytellers before anything else. That is our tradition, an ancient and honorable one going back to the fire pit in prehistory. Television and movies are the more recent venues of this lineage, but writers are the direct descendants of a time when narratives were memorized and passed from master to apprentice in the course of many generations. But over time, the process of storytelling has evolved. We are now illustrators too. We don't use the movie screen to do this, we use the visualization process in the reader's mind. Do we say, "He was running as fast as he could?" We might, or we could say, "He had to slow down to keep his lungs from bursting."

At the leading edge of any plot we have the setup. This is where you enter from the edge of the map, which is also the top of your word processor page. Here we also encounter the reporter's four informational requirements for an opening paragraph: who, what, when and where. If not in the first paragraph, you must still establish these elements early, preferably within that first page, since the attention of a reader who does not know all of them will wander quickly. Keep your language dynamic and visual, but don't be afraid to handle some of your opening in this traditional manner, since your reader approaches your book with some expectations of her own. She wants to be grounded, anchored in the earliest phase of the story. Throwing her under the *avant-garde* bus in the first paragraph for stylistic reasons will not win you many friends or readers. The great experiments in writing from the early years of the twentieth century did not for the most part give birth to new and innovative styles. *Ulysses* and *Finnegan's Wake* of James Joyce set the standard for word play in fiction but are almost never read today. The chief beneficial effect of books like this, or those of Virginia Woolf, was to break free of Victorian restraints and to liberate new generations of younger writers by showing them the range of possibility that they faced. Much of their value to us was, ironically, negative. They freed us from a set of prim controls but did not usually point the direction to the future in any detail.

Keeping the reader from knowing enough to orient herself to your story is not a breakthrough in literary technique. To her, it will look more like arrogance or indifference. If the opening line is dialog, tell us who is speaking, what is the occasion, and when and where it's happening. This may seem mundane, and it is, but it is also the anchor that holds the story in place before it takes off under its own power. While you have already worked out all of this in your own mind, to the reader it is new and strange terrain. Hold her hand for a while before you cast her loose into the briar patch of your drama. Establish some trust, because she needs to be engaged over the long and dangerous journey you are asking her to share with you. Part of her courage derives from being confident that you know what you're doing. Don't demonstrate to her on page one that you do not.

In this opening chapter you will also establish the problem. It can be nearly anything of significant magnitude that invites the pursuit of a solution, which is another name for your road map, the plot. At this point you must be able to answer this question for each of your characters: what does this person want? What or who is preventing him from getting it? This will drive his actions, and in turn, your plot.

In mysteries, it usually revolves around a crime. The quest for the solution is to know "who done it," and the apprehension of that person, the criminal or perp, is the problem. Each chapter needs to be one in a series of obstacles to that solution. Even as they increase in difficulty, they should appear to be getting closer.

In other kinds of fiction, such as romance, it can be the finding of a person to love or the salvaging of a relationship nearly lost. In war novels, like Norman Mailer's *The Naked and the Dead*, or Joseph Heller's *Catch-22*, it can be the survival of the individual as a functioning entity trapped in the dehumanizing crucible of war. It can be any resolution that appeals to you, but no matter what the level of detail you employ in the planning phase of your book, you should be aware, at least in general terms, what that solution is before you put your pen to paper. This is your endpoint, and you need to keep it in view.

If it is biography or autobiography, the reader must come away feeling that this was a life with meaning, a life that made (or makes) sense to the person living it and the people around him. The opening question is then more about how this life is going to go, how early obstacles are overcome. How did this person transcend his background and the times he grew up in to reach a resolution that gave meaning to the conflict in the process?

Why should he now be an example for others? Or, conversely, if the life runs off the rails, the reader must see it as the tragedy of unrealized potential and understand why it happened.

You will remember that the reader has embarked on a detailed journey with you. The principal reason she is coming along and adding her own feelings and insights to the story is that she can see the need for this solution just as well as you do. If you don't provide it in a satisfying way at the end, you will have misled her and she won't be back for the sequel or any other books of yours. Meeting her needs, and understanding why she came along, is called *respecting your reader*. We've seen this before, and it is part of the writer's ethic. We'll take this up again in Chapter 18, Handling the Truth.

Knowing where the story ends, the final point

on this map, is fundamental to figuring out how to get there. For inexperienced writers the best approach to this lies either in an outline or a chapter-by-chapter synopsis. In setting this up, you need not include every detail, only those events which move other events. Think of them as pivot points. A single chapter synopsis will have some of the same features as the book concept does. It will start with a strong opening, hopefully the best sentence of the chapter. If you know it, put this in the synopsis so you don't lose track of it. The function of this being the best sentence is that the reader will feel compelled to read the next one. You should always have the intention, in a subtle way, of creating suspense as you go. It need not be the kind of suspense that asks who is going to jump out of the closet and stab the main character. It can be as subtle as, "I wonder why she did that? Is there something I'm not seeing yet?" The logical response is to read further—the essence of literary suspense.

In this sense, every novel is a mystery—the reader stays with it to find out what happens to the characters you have drawn well enough to engage her. Your job is to also get her sufficiently invested in the story at the beginning to make her stay with it. To do that you must keep her asking questions.

One aspect to look at in a series of chapter

synopses is what and how much information is revealed at each step—where does it lead the reader? Surprises are a bonus, but they are better when they have a basis in the prior information you've provided. If your plot is bogged down, then a surprise can jumpstart the action. Remember that each chapter needs to have a specific function on the plot map. You ought to be able to sum up its purpose in a single line with a statement like this: Chapter Four reveals for the first time that Leo is Amy's father (naturally in the final line). This will raise yet another dilemma for Chapter Five—since as it moves forward, Chapter Four supplies only obstacles, not solutions, even as it provides this information. In this case, Amy can't deal with it and has an emotional breakdown and runs away on the last page of Five. Then Chapter Six, concerning itself with tracking her down, hits a dead end following a thread that had appeared promising, and so on.

Somewhere in an earlier passage you will have shown us that Leo has an interest in Amy that makes us wonder what his intentions are. After all, there's a substantial age difference between them. The reader suspects it might be slightly inappropriate, although these relationships happen, but when their kinship is revealed, it simultaneously surprises her and confirms her instincts, because you have laid the groundwork for it. This is called foreshadowing, and it is both a useful and a necessary tool in fiction. Don't fail to employ it. It works best when the foreshadowing, as above, does not suggest the exact outcome once it appears. It leaves the reader thinking that she *knew* something was going on, but not exactly what. She can feel slightly ahead of the author without having gotten it perfectly right. This is a win-win situation for the author, because the reader is staying at the cutting edge of the story, but not anticipating the outcome at every turn.

This raises another point. I don't mind letting the reader feel like she's gotten ahead of me from time to time. For one thing, this affirms her engagement with the plot and characters. In my mysteries I use a first person point of view narrator, and occasionally a chapter cast in the third person to bring in needed information from the outside. Naturally, my narrator can only know what he sees himself. If the reader is jumping up and down because of something she knows that he doesn't, and she's saying, "No, no, don't open that door!" then she is deeply involved and feeling that she's running slightly ahead of the narrator as well. There's nothing wrong with that, and it's just as good a process of engagement as suspense. In the same spirit as varying the pace, I try to use both. Readers are often eager to tell me, with a big smile, the exact moment when they guessed who the killer was.

An old theater adage is that if you introduce a gun onstage in the first act you must fire it by the third. In addition to foreshadowing, this illustrates one other element. The reader does not take kindly to red herrings. Even if it has a relaxed feel, your book must still be crafted as a tight fabric, one with a structure that is not entirely visible to the reader. Don't bring in an element as specific and as dangerous as a gun without having it play an important role in the story. I don't mean a gun like any cop would naturally carry, walking across the intersection outside the window. I'm talking about the Sig Sauer Nine that your character discovers hidden behind the antique French marble clock over the fireplace. He covers his mouth in surprise. If you don't find an honest and necessary role for this firearm later, the reader will feel manipulated, and therefore, disrespected. Remember, she is invested in this story too. She is helping you build it, layer by layer, as we talked about in Chapter 5, The Reader's Role. Her ongoing commitment to your labor is one of your most valuable assets, and the only way your book becomes a joint effort. A red herring will be correctly perceived to have only one purpose—to deceive your readers.

In working out the twists and turns of your story it is useful to remember that not every moment can be dramatic. The ones that aren't function as a way to vary the pace, a necessary feature, but otherwise only exist to advance the story in the way you would drive from one point to another. It has to be done to change the scene, but the road may be smooth and the weather sunny and warm because you don't need a crisis in the story at that point. Don't waste any more time with these situations than you have to in order to let the reader know the facts. I think of them as facilitating scenes, ones that tell your reader the nuts and bolts of what she needs to know, but don't expect her to be deeply engaged by them, so move on quickly. Don't waste time describing some midpoint of this journey in great detail when it plays no role in the action.

It will be the more dramatic scenes that drive your movement through the plot roadmap. The key to this is conflict, not only among characters, but *inside* the characters. This is the chief reason we have no interest in stereotypical players in our story—not only are they uninteresting on the surface, but they don't have the complexity to experience conflict within. How does this kind of conflict work?

Think of those occasions when you were unable to make a decision on an important matter. Two or more forces were pulling at you with enough strength to cancel each other, to neutralize your will to go forward. In your mind you could construct a plausible case to go either way, but you can't seem to locate a deciding factor to tip the scales. This is the situation you want to place your characters in from time to time. The effect is greatly enhanced when you add the pressure of a time limit factor. It's like a locomotive driving down the rails. Do you jump to the right or to the left if you're in its path? Negative consequences exist on either side. The steam seems to mount in the character's head. An effective way to resolve this crisis is to throw in an unexpected element that blows the scene wide open. If it provides a third, unexpected choice, all the better, especially if that choice is taken without much analysis in the stress of the moment. This can also be a fine time to end the chapter with an implicit question mark that opens the door for further complications in the following chapter. These are the unintended consequences, and in mysteries, they often lead to the second and even the third, murder. Always pay attention to the logic of events as you work out these details. All children and many adults believe that their actions have no consequences. This is called wishful thinking. The knowledge that the opposite is true is one of your principal plotting tools.

Look again at your plot map. Any flashback will appear as a swampy detour, sending your reader off the track into unknown and unexpected terrain, where her momentum will be lost while she sloshes along at two miles an hour through the mud. Don't expect her to thank you for this; she was doing quite well going seventy on the main road as your story moved steadily ahead. She enjoys the feeling of the wind in her hair as you unwind the plot. Slowing her down to feed her background information will make her impatient and she will pay less attention than you would like to what you're trying to tell her. If the information in the flashback is important, you need to have introduced it in a better way, perhaps by working it into a conversation in smaller bits. If it's not that important, just forget about it. Make it a priority to organize your material in a way that doesn't require flashbacks. If they are absolutely necessary, try to do them in tiny segments, so they are almost unnoticed as they're absorbed like scenery. Especially in this case, more is definitely less. Live by it. Just because you know things about your character doesn't mean your reader needs to as well. Some of the information you have was mainly helpful in building those characters when you first began to sketch them out, but doesn't add to the action once it's in motion.

An effective map will, however, still have many crossroads and forks in the road. They are not flashback slowdowns, but only a miniscule pause in which to decide whether to go left, right, or stay the course. Since they elevate the pressure, crossroads are decision points for your characters. Their arrival should sometimes be surprising, but not always, and they should be accompanied by an appropriate degree of uncertainty and tension. It is permitted that your reader might have her own view of what choice should've been made, once it is, even when it's not what your character chose. To maintain your suspense, some forks in the road will not be visible until the character arrives there and slams on the brakes to scan his options. If he sees a directional sign, it's probably disfigured by graffiti. The best place to introduce these obstacles is at the end of a chapter. Here's an example:

Imagine that your reader is in bed with your book. It's a little past her normal time to turn out the light, but she has stayed with the chapter because there's a chase scene going on. Her need is for an outcome so she can ease off to sleep without wondering what's about to happen. In a word, she wants resolution! In the story your main character is pursuing two others, but he can't quite catch up to them. His own desperate need is to get an answer to a question, one pivotal to the plot, but he doesn't know which of the people he's chasing can supply it. Suddenly a fork in the road appears, and each of the fleeing characters takes a different route.

End of chapter, period, but your reader's pulse is still uncomfortably elevated.

As the writer you have now gotten the roadmap right. Ignoring the fact that she has a report to deliver to the board of directors at 9:15 in the morning, your reader utters a deep sigh and turns the page to the next chapter. This is where having the best sentence in that chapter come first is going to pay off. She has chosen you over the need for a good night's sleep before an important meeting. Don't feel bad; it's a competitive world. Having a loyal reader choose you and your story is never a bad thing.

Clearly, effective chapter endings display your talent as a persuader, a fundamental aspect of storytelling. When I was a little kid going to Saturday matinee movies at the Camden Theater in North Minneapolis, the second part of the presentation, after a Warner Brothers cartoon, was always a serial.

I particularly remember *Don Winslow of the Navy*. I think it must have originally been a comic book—even in film it had that graphic look—although I never saw a pulp version. The serial always ended with a cliffhanger that usually had something to do with a Nazi destroyer and depth charges. I'm sure the staff screenwriter with the most dependable instincts wrote the final two minutes of all of them. As the credits rolled while I was still gasping, I couldn't wait for the next one, to see what happened.

The point was simple and effective. The theater owner rented those serials because he could depend on them to bring the kids back the following week to see what was going to happen next. The feature-length movie that followed on each bill ran for seven days and it was not a serial, so, although it may have had its own kind of impact, it didn't have this power from one week to the next. The man in the front office was buying continuity.

Your task is no different. You don't need to have the oxygen shutting down and the lights failing as the sub is pitching nose first toward the bottom, out of control and even now beyond its maximum safe operating depth. Soon it will be crushed like an eggshell during a cattle stampede. Times are different now, as is your audience. Some subtlety is in order, even though the fundamental task has not changed. It is to persuade the reader to sprint across that stretch of blank page to the head of the next chapter, and entice her to begin again.

But how is that done? One way is to withhold something from the chapter's closing narrative, such as: at what maximum depth can the submarine survive? Surely it can't resurface. The viewer sees no options, nor does your reader. If an epidemic is approaching and people are dropping like flies, maybe this is the time to reveal that Amy had a mild case as a child in Malaysia and is now immune, even as her brother, born in California three years later, is slipping away with beads of sweat rolling off his brow. His lips are moving—is he about to say his final words? Perhaps he knows who his own father is, and it's not Leo! Often it is some small detail connected to the road map that shows the way. Watch for the signs. You will want to be subtler than I've been in this paragraph, since I have overdrawn it to make my point. As I have addressed in another part of this book, don't let the reader see you moving the scenery around. She'll feel manipulated.

Here's another example that provides a hook simply based on foreshadowing. It's the final paragraph of a chapter from my book, *The Amarna*

Heresy, where the character Alex Beck emerges after an amazing conversation:

It was a powerful idea, possibly the most powerful single idea she'd ever had. Standing on a dingy back street in Luxor, where competing mule carts and battered pickups made two street lanes out of one, Alex's vision broadened to include a wider slice of the world than she'd ever taken in before, which may have explained why she didn't notice the blind man in an ancient wicker wheelchair huddled against the front wall of the cafe she had emerged from. A man who, even while he lifted his cup in mute and hopeless supplication to passersby, turned to watch her walk away through his dark glasses. After all, eye disease is everywhere in Egypt. Like the mounds of limestone rubble at every turn, no one notices it after a while. There are so many other things, great and memorable things, to look at.

Now the end of your book looms only twenty thousand words off. You can feel the climax in your throat like a peach pit. It might even be a little too big and ragged to handle, although you have been gaining momentum page by page. Here is where having the map pays off once again, because you can see the route this far, and you already know the end, so it's a matter of maintaining suspense as you are connecting the dots. It's time to look over your work and see if all your chapters are working in the same direction, pushing toward the same goal. If you've been revising continuously, (see Revision), you are well equipped to do this because the material is still familiar in your mind. You should be able to articulate a reason in each chapter that explains why the protagonist was not able to achieve his goals. Sometimes the obstacles are no more than physical, but don't underestimate them. Setting is mood, atmosphere, and, yes, the geography of your roadmap. Always take a closer look to confirm that it reinforces plot, because as we'll see in the next chapter, its effectiveness depends on how it's used.

A final word concerning pace. We have heard that heart-thumping rhythm is a vital element in almost any kind of fiction. I remarked elsewhere that bestselling authors are often no more than good pacers. Do not, however, become obsessive about pace and make your manuscript a one-note samba. Nonstop action is like eating an entire meal of chocolate. You may think that sounds good, but it doesn't take long to become too much, sending you searching for the broccoli and the sauerkraut.

As I've suggested above now and then, successful pace is built on variety. Break-neck pace becomes invisible if not interrupted periodically. If you don't give the reader a chance to breathe between scenes, your plot will seem all the same, and she'll grow tired and bored even at the most hectic points. She will need to rest periodically, to digest what you have shown her, and to breathe easier, but don't make the mistake of thinking that the insertion of a flashback here is a good place for her to do this.

The color red in a painting is usually a focal point, but an entirely red painting is no more than a bloody bore. In art, we'd use a bit of green to *pop* the red and make it stand out. The variation in pace acts the same way in writing.

9.

THE SETTING

Memorably, Gertrude Stein once remarked about Oakland, California, her home town, "There is no there there." I always interpreted this as meaning, in her wry prose style, that it lacked a distinctive sense of place, which explains why she spent most of her life in Paris. It brought to mind the real estate agent's mantra, "Location, location, location."

Next to the defect of not telling the reader early on who is speaking, why, and when, the absence of a specific location is high on my list of dangerous omissions. If you imagine that your characters are moving about on a stage of your making, then the lack of props and backgrounds would place the actors in limbo—two or three people on the concrete floor of a warehouse whose walls have disappeared from view in the darkness. The barred prison windows at the ceiling are too high to matter. Overhead, a single naked light bulb illuminates the scene. This would only be appropriate if you're specifically suggesting alienation and detachment. However, *Waiting for Godot* and other minimalist dramas have been done, quite effectively, and as a novelist it is not your task to replicate them. An absence of background in your book suggests not alienation in the characters but bungling in the author. Your reader is eager to fill in the details of your set—give her a specific framework to hang them on.

In a larger sense, location is part of *context*, which in the case of fiction includes all sense impressions plus the emotional condition of the actors. If your characters are passing a slaughterhouse, imagine the sounds and smells coming from inside. Your visual description of a neatly kept brick exterior can contrast markedly with the meatpacking business. If your plot includes an impending disaster, a jarring, contradictory setting like this can foreshadow it.

In my book, *The Amarna Heresy*, four of my characters are fleeing across the Wadi Rum desert in Jordan in a stolen thirty-year-old Bentley:

Three young archaeologists and a recent widow gravely scanned the looming, broken landscape of the cliffs. No grace of the Rockies or the Alps appeared, with their tapering peaks in aspects of blue and purple laced in white;

here the formations ranged long and hori-
zontal, striated with more red and brownish
courses that continued until the outcroppings
fractured into rubble and disappeared into the
sand. Beyond and out of view, others backed
them in chaotic rows. It was a landscape of
conflict, of unresolved violence. It seemed to each
of the travelers a fit place for four people fleeing for their lives. The distance offered sudden
glimpses of green and watery mirages that had
tempted even Lawrence of Arabia in these desperate marches, but had never for even a moment
existed. And Lawrence had the local Bedou-
ins to guide him; these fugitives had only their
stubborn wits.

Notice the way the description evokes the
mood; it's not just local color.

In another hour they were approaching
the gap. The shale had soon sunk back under
the surface, and Tech was reduced to following camel trails where he could find them. The
wind-blown sand picked up speed again and
sheets of it whispered over the car and collected
on the windshield wipers and in the air ducts.

The sun had moved higher in the sky, and within the car, the air was close. Their faces grew moist and eager as they opened the windows a slit on the leeward side.

The whisper of the wind, the moisture collecting on their skin, the broken landscape of the wind-rotted cliffs all set the scene. You can almost hear the crunch of the tires going over the shale fragments in the sand. The setting becomes an active and hostile character as the drama unfolds.

Against this dominant locale you can play out the dialog. It is one where fear duels with the need to appear to be brave and seem almost normal under intense stress. The setting can either underline the conversation, or contrast with it. Better yet, it can go back and forth. Without the unremitting presence of the desert, it would only be four people out for a drive in a classic car.

When is it appropriate to use a setting like this? The four characters are being pursued by people trying to kill them. Given any casual mistake, the desert will also bring them down. The terrain they're crossing has no roads, so they don't know with any exactness where they are. The old Bentley may make it or not. It's well-constructed, but thirty is not a good age for any vehicle. They have enough water to make it across in the car, but not enough if the car fails, or if they're stopped by the landscape. The terrain could change at any time, and the wind may be covering their trail or not, laying them open to being followed. Their greatest need is certainty, the element least available to them.

I traveled to Egypt and Jordan to research this book, walking the trails I placed my characters on. I visited tombs in the Valley of the Kings and hung out in the smoke-filled restaurants of back alley Luxor. Before I went I had already written half of it, including conversations in places I had no backdrop for until I saw them. The dialog changed once I filled in the settings. It is a novel where the setting is one of the main characters.

The point is that the setting reinforces the action simply by being there in the way it's portrayed. It needs to be part of the emotional fabric of the story. Don't overlook the possibility of using the setting to boost tension as it thwarts the desires of your characters. You would not include a setting like this desert scene merely for local color if it didn't advance the plot. It supplies mood, tension, and texture during a space in the book where four people are escaping from one place to another in a condition of doubt and fear. One of them is nearly a stranger to the others. The threatening overtones of the environment foreshadow the coming showdown when the bad guys catch up with them down the road. Set among the Roman theater ruins of Amman, Jordan, another dramatic setting, that confrontation is the climax of the novel.

In contrast, a calm element like snow can dominate and inform an entire story as in Graham Greene's *Orient Express* (published in England as *Stamboul Train*), and Orhan Pamuk's *Snow*.

Settings like these are frames for the action. As with a painting, the frame can enhance the effect on the canvas or it can add nothing. If inappropriate or insensitively done, it can detract or even distract from the painting. Its absence, as in the case of many unframed pictures hanging on people's walls, constitutes at best a series of lost opportunities. As the author, you must be on top of all the detail to bring your reader into your setting. When I was researching backgrounds in Egypt and Jordan, I returned with more than 400 photos I could reference as I worked. The sense impression of it I brought back in my notes. That kept the detail accessible and real.

I can't stress enough the value of spending some time in the settings you write about. Open your senses to the smells, sights, and sounds. The entire ambience can become part of your story, indeed, one of your characters.

10.

DIALOG

"Hey!"

"'Sup?"

"Not much."

"How's it goin'?"

"Can't complain."

"What's shakin'?"

Despite all the quotation marks, none of the above lines constitutes dialog, since they carry no content. In the discipline of Rhetoric they're called phatic utterances. Part of greeting behavior, like hand gestures and fake kisses, they act as preliminary markers to a conversation that may or may not develop when two people meet. In terms of this chapter, they are mainly of interest because they illustrate what dialog is not.

One of the chief values of dialog lies in its immediacy. To use a film shot as a metaphor, it is our close up. It contains both information and behavior delivered face to face. You will not witness a dialog from half a mile away. It can be gestural, contradictory, deceptive, or it can demonstrate any number of other characteristics. It offers the reader a way of getting into the heads of actors that are not narrators, and whose point of view is not used directly in the story. Carefully done, it brings the characters involved into sharp focus as nothing else can.

Several years ago I read Ian McEwan's fine novel, *Atonement*. It was a bestseller and was subsequently made into a popular movie. I enjoyed it, but on finishing it I was puzzled by one thing: the strangely infrequent use of dialog. I could go for page after page without coming across a single line. Dialog was simply not one of the important tools the author relied on. I raise this issue because that experience underlined for me how important dialog normally is in fiction. I have to say, that as good a book as *Atonement* is, I think it would be significantly better with more dialog. I came away with an unwelcome sense of the distance between the characters and myself. Seeing them more in conversation could have cured that. Be that as it may, I'm sure McEwan had his own good reasons for constructing the book that way; possibly to emphasize some of the characters' isolation from each other, or the abstractness of the moral wrong that occurred. It may also reflect his interest in metafiction, a technique where the writing ironically calls attention to itself, but that's beyond the scope of this chapter. In any case, without being more judgmental, I'm going to recommend that you do the exact opposite.

A tradition runs through American entertainment media that suggests drama is best illustrated by violence. The video game tradition is firmly anchored in this. Going back, it may have its roots in the Indian Wars, or the gunfights of the Old West. It continues in westerns and cop shows today. In the late fifties and into the sixties, when a new wave of European films began to find an audience in the United States, they illustrated a startling difference in approach, displaying a vast range of dramatic situations carried and delivered by dialog. Perhaps World War II had made Europeans sick to death of violence and they sought ways to find drama in the more subtle exchanges between people facing each other with no weapons beyond their wits.

Drama in dialog springs from the unexpected. If I arrive on your doorstep in the hope of selling you a life insurance policy, but you mistake me for a social worker who's coming to prepare your aged mother psychologically to go off to assisted living that afternoon, we are likely to have a lively conversation that fails to connect. Its dynamic is based on misunderstanding. The writer will want to continue the misunderstanding as long as it serves his purpose, because when it is resolved, the scene will end. This is accomplished when neither party states his intentions or assumptions. If the scene ends without resolution, then you have a cliffhanger chapter ending.

Conversations between two characters who both already understand and agree on the information they're going to exchange may be revealing or necessary to inform the reader—in which case they are best kept brief—but they are not likely to be dramatic, and drama fuels the momentum of your story. It they go on too long, your reader will be looking at her watch, wondering whether this might be a good place to stick the bookmark back in and turn out the light. Her thumb feathers over the next few pages, as she wonders how long this goes on. Make no mistake, she is looking for action.

The best conversations involve two people who want different things and do not understand each other. They enter with mistaken assumptions, as we have seen above. This kind of conflict, rather than violence, is the true basis of drama that sustains the reader's interest because it is a source of anxiety on both sides. If my need is to sell you life insurance, and you keep sending me into your mother's bedroom for a quiet talk with her about her future needs, I am not going to be able to meet my present need, and as long as this misunderstanding continues, then we have a drama. Meanwhile your frustration is mounting because you need to get your mother packed to leave and you can't understand why I'm not helping. Perhaps this is the moment for the doorbell to ring and you to find the real social worker on the front step. If you need to extend the confusion further, then your character can refuse to recognize her credentials, or perhaps she doesn't have them along with her, and we'll have more misunderstanding.

With this in mind, as the writer you will need to plan conversations with a clear comprehension of what each character needs and wants. Tension can be created when neither recognizes, understands, or simply accepts, what the other's need is. Word meanings become slippery in this context. Here's a snippet from a scene from the first of my mysteries, *Twenty Centavos*. The subject, Barbara Watt, has just arrived to pose for Paul Zacher, the artist turned detective. He is a man who is serious in his studio; he is at work, just as surely as if he were at his office:

I led Barbara up to the studio and pointed out a screen at the end by the south windows. "You can change there. There's a robe on the hook, I think." There was the sound of clothes being pulled off and she emerged a moment later in Maya's silk robe and stood by the easel. Then she untied the robe and dropped it to the floor.

"What do you think?" She held out her hands.

"Stunning." I was pulling out tubes of paint. "What were you thinking about for a pose?"

"Stunning? Just like that? I'm standing here naked and you just say, 'stunning'? Don't you want to...you know, touch me just a little? Maya's not here, is she? I hoped we could have a *rendezvous*."

"Barbara," I said, squeezing out some titanium white onto my pallet, "please don't think I'm not appreciating you. You're really gorgeous. But painting is just not an erotic activity for me. I tend to look at the human body as a kind of landscape; a few hills here, some valleys there, an outcropping or two of bush." I meant this.

"Look at me!" There was an edgy, demanding tone in her voice.

Notice the ongoing activity on both sides during this encounter. It forms a detailed counterpoint to the dialog. Imagine your characters on stage doing some *business* as they talk. Unless it's a deathbed scene, keep them both moving. We want to witness the nuance of their body language, which is a critical part of this or any conversation. The characters' movements and gestures can either support or contradict what they're saying, depending on the effect you're trying to achieve. Activity that undermines the dialog can be a great source of tension. In this passage, notice the narrator's insistence on normalcy, not revealed by what he says as much as his continued involvement in the routine task of squeezing paint out of a tube onto his palette. Artist's oils are expensive, and he wants to introduce the right amount, but no more than he has to. Meanwhile Barbara Watt is offering what she feels is a crescendo of great skin and opportunity. They are on a completely different wavelength. The outcome of this disconnect is drama.

How do your characters interact with their environment? Do they experience the smells and sounds around them? Do these elements affect their mood? You can see how awkward it would be if they were both standing there doing nothing but saying their lines in the scene above. Think of them as actors employed by you, the writer-director in sole charge of the action.

Since this dialog does not occur at the end of the book, but close to the beginning, it does not resolve in a satisfactory way for either Barbara Watt, or Paul Zacher, the narrator/painter. The partial resolution it provides advances the story by setting the backdrop for Barbara's ongoing pursuit of Paul, and his investigation of key members of the expat community as he tries to solve the murder of a prominent antiques dealer.

Partial resolution of these dialog segments is the norm. They are present in part to convey the reader into the next conflict and misunderstanding, the next obstacle between the main character and the solving of the case or the story's problem. Each encounter reveals more, but never all, until the final scene.

Because most of my books are set in México, an issue arises about dialect, a common element in dialog, and one often mishandled. I was aware of the pitfalls from the beginning, since many of my characters do not speak English as their first language. How was I to show that, without constant misspellings and contractions? Putting down pidgin English on your page illustrates how easy it is to overdo, and ends up calling attention to itself at the expense of more important parts of the action. I decided to go with a concept I'd learned in painting: if you are depicting a tree, do not show every leaf. Find a shorthand that represents them *en masse*, and when you do show individual leaves, make each one unique.

A San Miguel judicial cop named Diego Delgado has a prominent role in many of my mysteries. When he attempts to speak English, the trick is to convey the foreignness of his construction without changing the pronunciation of the words as written. The reader already understands that Delgado has an accent; there is no need to illustrate in each word. Here he is with Paul Zacher in *The Book Doctor* at breakfast, talking about the condition of a client manuscript that the murdered book doctor (Justus Barlow) had in his hotel room. Zacher speaks first, and notice Delgado's response.

"Barlow's treatment of it was no different from the others. The pages had been roughly handled, full of stains and creases. I recall a pinfeather stuck to the top of page four like an exclamation point. The markings were all in blunt pencil, many of them illegible."

"Yet this Señor Barlow was a professional, no? How could this be? He did not have the pride of his job?"

The question reflects a Méxican's sensitivity to a proper appearance in business, but it is the nuance of the word order in Delgado's comment that tells us all we need to know about how he said it. His phrasing in no way demeans his intelligence. Anything more, in my view, would be obtrusive.

There is another risk inherent in dialect. It tends to reflect unconscious prejudices about the speaker. Think of the Uncle Remus stories of Joel Chandler Harris. They originally appeared in the nineteenth century, but were revived by Walt Disney in the mid-twentieth. Their dialect is broad and prominent, and probably derives from minstrel shows and later, vaudeville. It reflects the white man's take on African American speech patterns, and it didn't take long before it was perceived as offensive. An element of this same condescension can easily slip into almost any bit of dialect offered by someone of a different culture. It has always been a trap to watch for in my treatment of Méxicans. I have great affection and regard for the people of México, but I also harbor unconscious American cultural biases that can get past me unnoticed in small ways if I'm not careful.

A better course, for a variety of reasons, is to simply suggest the differences in word order or colloquialisms, without dwelling on them.

I recently reread *A Catcher in the Rye*, after many years. It was always a book I recalled fondly from the great tradition of coming-of-age fiction. On this rendition I found myself irritated by what I thought of as the overuse of midcentury teenage hip dialect. By the second decade of the twenty-first century, this language is so dated that, for me, it does little more than call attention to itself. This tends to obstruct its meaning and to exaggerate its importance in the paragraph by giving it an unwanted prominence. Its original cutting edge impact has now been lost.

The problem with using slang in your book is that it changes at a far faster rate than conventional language, and therefore becomes harder to understand as the distance increases from the time it was written. Much of the fashionable chatter people used with each other in the twenties is now incomprehensible. When did you last say to someone, "23 skidoo?" How many of us could even guess what it means?

The best solution is again the kind of short-hand that will suggest the differences from conventional speech, without intruding itself like a speed bump in the dialog. This will not date as easily, and properly done, will never appear condescending.

Borrow a note from the theater here, because your book is playing in the theater of your reader's mind. You may witness the flash of lightning and hear the thunder on the stage, but the real drama is carried by the dialog among the characters you see and the immediacy of their gestures and movements, the "business" that they're doing. This physical aspect of dialog can either reinforce or contradict the meaning of what is said, and is no less a part of the scene than the words. For the writer, dialog is often a song and a dance performed together.

A friend of mine who is an established screen-writer once showed me a screenplay he had finished. I was astonished at how bare it was of cues for the characters or settings. It was all left to the actors and the director to fill in. As the writer of fiction, these important tasks are left to you.

11.

VOICE AND TONE

Often we start out as novice writers using a style we hope resembles that of our favorite novelist. We think that if only we could write like he does, we'd be nothing short of great. By the time I was a high school junior I had read and admired many of William Faulkner's books. I thought I understood his technique, his word choices, his quirky punctuation, and his choice of characters. I could have made a long list of attributes that distinguished his work from that of other writers. He was hugely successful, and had won the Nobel Prize in 1950.

His platform grew out of two elements. One was his early Twentieth Century upbringing—he was born in 1897. His beginnings were embedded in the South of Reconstruction; the embittered, battered, but stubbornly undefeated South, with its red dirt matrix of racism and poverty. The pretension of its decayed aristocracy. An important Alabama author once said to me that it was a breeding ground for story-tellers who mined a rich tradition as they continuously picked apart and rewove the loose ends of history for their purposes. Faulkner had left that Mississippi to spend a portion of 1925 in Paris, then a crucible of literary innovation and a caldron of change for all the arts. This gave him the impetus to experiment. The timing and fusion of these two elements brought to his style and outlook the unique flavor that made him famous.

It will be no surprise when I say that my prose style came to resemble his as closely as I could make it, at least in my own mind. At that time of my life I had never visited the South. There was no possible way I could evoke the background to properly capture Faulkner's mood, and we have already seen that the setting needs to be a major character in our books.

Well, you say, what did Faulkner's books have to do anyway with a teenager from Minnesota who wanted to learn to write? An excellent question, but one for which I can furnish no good answer, other than that it was more likely only one of many steps forward, this one near of the bottom of the staircase.

Part of this is merely the process of modeling, a way of learning. Your father can explain to you at dinner how to pound a nail into a piece of wood, but watching him do it later out on the workbench in the garage is a better way to learn. You see the nuance of his grip on the hammer, the way his thumb aligns with the top of the handle. You observe the way he places the nail at its precise entry point and taps it lightly to set it in place. You watch how each swing of the hammer gets more powerful, and you witness the unwavering alignment of his eye with the nail's head. And then comes the final blow that sets it flush with the surface of the wood. It is just enough to leave no hammer mark behind. Few ways of picking up a skill are this effective.

Another aspect of mimicry as learning is that everyone knows William Faulkner was brilliant, so if my work reads somewhat like his, then I must be at least very good too, right?

But imitation is like taking baby steps, a necessary process, but one soon outdated. We have had our William Faulkner, now more than fifty years dead, and we don't need any imitations. No matter how good they seem to be, they will always be no more than pale replicas. Imagine even a highly skilled painter making a copy of a van Gogh that had sold for $40 million. What is it worth, even if it's so good that it's distinguishable only by an expert? It might be valued at two or three hundred dollars.

This process is often what happens on a writer's first book. It is certainly a way of learning about style and voice from a successful author's work, which is beneficial as an example of what one writer did, but it is not likely to produce a competent or salable manuscript. If you are constantly working with one eye on what William Faulkner would be saying in this or that paragraph, as I was, you will be neglecting what your character needs to be saying or doing, and more important, what you would be saying or doing as an author true to his own vision. You cannot borrow someone else's thunder. The risk in trying is that you may have only one book in you, so if you are frustrated or disappointed with the outcome, you may find yourself lost in mimicry, and finished with your writing career before you have properly begun.

By *tone*, one of my chapter title words above, I mean your individual identity as expressed on the page. You might also call it voice. Like that of Faulkner, yours is unique, and it is composed of elements every bit as legitimate and worthwhile in their origins as his were. But for you to find and develop that voice, you must understand its roots, you must nurture them, and you must have the courage to speak with honesty. You must own *all* of your own history, even when it includes your demons as well as your strengths—perhaps especially then. Were the great writers you have read always working from the most successful moments of their lives? I would say that's more like rarely the case. They worked from their pain and embarrassment, their frustration and their longing. Embracing all the elements of your *self* is the keystone of insight and true knowledge. In writing, its use will not always or even often be in the form of autobiography, but this voice will be heard in the way your characters connect and interact, the responses they have to events in their lives and to their environment, and in the inevitability of what happens to them in the end.

If you grew up as an only child in a close, loving family of fisher folk in a seacoast town in New Brunswick, and your principal character is a rogue stock trader in Cape Town, the ninth of fourteen children in a family of wasted alcoholics, you will still find that person within yourself, distilled (no pun here), assembled, and reconfigured from your own experience. It is the confidence in what you have learned in life, from your family and friends, your lovers, your business associates, and your children that gives you the resources to write this character. You will have seen more about this idea in the earlier chapter titled: Getting Inside Yourself.

My fundamental point is that the uses of imitation have their natural limits. Put this process aside as quickly as you can, since even though it may make you feel like a writer, it impedes your task of knowing yourself well enough to speak from the heart, *your* heart, and in your own voice. Mimicking the voice of another writer is like wearing a mask on a first date. It makes your partner uneasy. Your self when concealed or veiled does not have the appeal of even your quirky self when revealed. This means with courage, with honesty, and with the conviction that people will want to hear what you have to say, even when it makes them uncomfortable. Not all of them will, but not everyone reads Faulkner, either. As writers our task is to find our unique audience, and to do that we must present ourselves as we really are, because the connection between reader and writer is an intimate one. We have allowed our reader access to our minds in a way few other occupations do. But even with our rags, bones, and warts, we are all still human, and the substance of our work is the way our humanity is expressed in our individuality and that of our characters. This is the true *voice* and *tone* of what we place on our pages.

Have we ever heard anyone described as one

of the great imitators of all time? Probably not. Good imitators are clever, and they may be skillful, but having spent their lives being someone else, they are not well remembered once they have departed the scene and their borrowed identity. Nor are they *ever* great.

Consider this for a moment, who was William Faulkner imitating? There is an excellent reason why no answer comes to mind.

12.

POINT OF VIEW

Point of view is one of the most subjective and difficult aspects of the craft to handle well. It involves making a decision about whose eyes your reader will use to witness the story. You will need to make a carefully considered decision about this before you put the first word to paper. There are several possibilities, each with different merits.

The first point of view to consider is Omniscient. You, as the narrator, know everything about the story and the characters, and all action is told in the third person. You may enter the thoughts of anyone. For the reader, this has an impersonal, godlike feel to it, which may put some readers off, and it has a tendency to be too objective, or too disengaged. You may have one sentence that tells what Ida is thinking, and the next sentence puts you inside Bill's mind. This feels like bouncing around, and it inhibits the process of the reader identifying with a character. I like to think of it as who I'm planning to hang my hat on when I'm reading a story, the one I'm going to connect with more than the others. Most readers will be "rooting" for one or another. That means they have found some similarities to connect with.

For myself, I like to feel I'm on approximately equal terms with the author. I'm neither student nor disciple, although I acknowledge that the writer is in charge of this journey. After writing eighteen books I now know within three paragraphs exactly what kind of book and author I'm looking at, and I prefer to think I'm striding side-by-side with the writer down the trail of the story. As you will remember from a previous chapter about the reasons movies can never replace books, identifying with a character has to do with leaving some "air" in the narrative fabric so the reader can insert her own thoughts and emotions. If the story is told by a godlike creature who knows every possible detail about it, the reader is less able to contribute to fill in these airy spaces, and therefore, to participate. And make no mistake; this participation is key to a reader's enjoyment of your work.

This is the reason I don't favor the Omniscient POV for myself. There may, however, be good reasons for your story to use it. Are you employing characters that are more or less than human?

Perhaps the characters are animals. Beings whose consciousness is inaccessible to normal minds like ours, and therefore need more explanation? In that case, only an omniscient narrator can plausibly get inside their heads, because the reader will have no experience of their kind of thinking. Is part of the story set at a great distance from the human characters, such as in a different galaxy or kind of existence that it's incomprehensible to those characters? Or is it a case of time travel, where human lifespans are too short to stretch between the past and present? These are some of the reasons you might want to look at Omniscient POV, because the other three have built-in limitations that may hamper concepts of this kind.

To use it merely to hop freely from one person's head to another, however, in a more conventional world, is to risk causing confusion and exasperation in the reader when done by a writer with less than first-rate skills.

Next, consider Third Person POV. This approach can use one or more characters to witness your story. One might be best, and usually no more than three or four should be used. Avoid picking too many, and select them for a particular strength they can bring to the narrative. The real trick is to shift gracefully among them. The ultimate goal is *clarity*; the reader must always know without much reflection who is talking or thinking. I can't stress this too much.

Some ways of showing the change from one POV to another are simple and can be done in the text. Skip a line between one person's view and another's. Or skip a line, add three asterisks and skip another. These are clear markers. I am currently reading Alison Lurie's *Truth and Consequences*, where she alternates chapters between the POV of the wife and that of the husband. Simple, traditional and effective. No question of clarity is possible. But often you don't want such a bold interruption of the narrative continuity when you change from one viewpoint to another.

In that case you can consider physical devices like separation of the characters. If Bill and Ida are part of a scene inside a room, looking out a window at a drama unfolding on the street, and we've been seeing the action through Ida's eyes, have her walk away. Maybe she leaves to answer the phone. In the next sentence, Bill continues to observe what's happening in the most natural manner possible, and the action is not interrupted for a second because the focus remains on the scene they were both watching. If it's well done, it will feel so seamless that most readers won't notice the change.

This raises a point I'd like to emphasize. Don't be a visible stagehand in your narrative, moving the furniture around, rolling up one backdrop and lowering another. You may be a character in your drama, but stay in character, even if you're the writer, as Somerset Maugham does, and don't let the audience see you unloading the trucks full of scenery and tweaking the lighting. One of the reasons we call writing a craft is that it's often more than a little bit *crafty*. Some sleight-of-hand and mental acrobatics are required.

I recently read Gore Vidal's *Lincoln*. Vidal was a great craftsman and handled POV with a smooth and informal hand. This book uses at least ten different ones—a tall order—and changes among talking heads are frequent. Usually no break at all is suggested between them beyond the mention of a character's name in a new paragraph. Because Vidal is so experienced and masterful, he still meets the standard of not confusing the reader, but an additional risk arises in this. I found I wanted to identify with *some* character in particular more than I did with any or all of them. For me, the book did not engage me fully, and it suffered because of that. It could be that Vidal thought of the POV as Omniscient, but if it was, why not get inside Lincoln's head too, practically the only major character he avoided? My sense of Omniscient would have required getting into Lincoln's POV above all the rest.

The story was interesting, the historical context was well crafted and plausible, but it came off as slightly too remote, and I ended it feeling less connected than I wanted to be. I realize that I usually avoid historical fiction—maybe this is the reason.

Next there is the rarely seen Second Person POV. I use it often, but not in any of my fiction. I find it can be an effective tool in a journalism piece. Here's an example from my blog, *Driving in Mexico II—Don't Drive While Married*:

Now you are slowly easing abreast of a herd of long-horned cattle edging the highway, when the possibility that something edible is clinging to the surface of your three-month-old maroon BMW is too much for them to ignore. Is it only the alpine meadow smell of Bavaria? Soon you are surrounded with creatures that have very big wet lips and rough dangling tongues that could remove the seal coat from your finish with a single exploratory lick. These are the same tongues that could sweep the spines from a cactus without a second thought. Your next move is one of near panic, as you...

The Second Person POV invites, almost compels, the reader to imagine herself behind the wheel. It's most effective in short spurts, and easily becomes tiresome as the POV of a long piece because it can come off as pushy. For book-length fiction or nonfiction, disregard it. If you're doing a blog post or writing a promo piece for your own book, take a hard look at it. It can have the immediacy of a one-on-one conversation when it comes off as insightful rather than imperative. Just to contradict what I said about using it in nonfiction, because this book is one of suggestion and instruction, I use it *intermittently* in these pages as a way of getting you to imagine yourself in a given situation.

For nuance and subtlety, I prefer the First Person POV. In reality, that's the POV of this book. When I use *you* in these paragraphs, often it is mostly in terms of a conversation we're having.

First, it offers a degree of intimacy not possible with the others. Reading a book is both a personal experience and a commitment. There are only two people involved, the reader and the author.

If the reader has gotten to page two, the relationship is already beginning to be one of trust, as it needs to be for the book to succeed. Naturally, this POV is the riskiest. You will need to strike a tone that is relatable, and I have written about tone and voice in another chapter. I said above that I, as a reader, need a character to hang my hat on. In a First Person POV, this can only be the narrator.

Here come the shades of gray again. For the writer, this is not only the most risky, it's the most exciting way to write a story—not an unusual combination. Even starting a book involves taking a big chance, so why not go for it? Yet, while I don't recommend multiple third person viewpoints for the inexperienced writer, the First Person POV is one that can be tackled right out of the gate. Why is that, when the writer has little experience and no exact idea of what he's trying to do?

I like it because the proper tone and style, once effectively established, can resonate with the reader, and when it does, require little tweaking to succeed throughout the book. It can be idiosyncratic without being bizarre or inaccessible. In short, it can be the way you think. Here's an example right off the top of my head:

"At the moment my older brother Joseph died, I was eating a strawberry ice cream in bright sunshine on a schoolyard swing two blocks away, at his school. There were three in the set. I was sitting in the middle one and I never used that one again, ever. Later, I felt I should've known something was dreadfully wrong, because we were always so close, but the truth was, I had no idea. When I did find out, two hours later..."

This character reveals many things about herself in these four sentences: guilt, self-revelation, a hint of family history, weather and season, the value of a close relationship as a source of insight. Notice that she displays no defensiveness about any of these. The next line or two will reveal her gender, although I think this already feels like a female narrator. Clearly, she was not there for Joseph in the way he must have been for her earlier. She is going to be our guide through this novel, probably a story of complex family relationships and the way they reverberated from her youth and beyond.

The key to pulling this off is that we need to find the narrator sympathetic—the sense that she, whether immediately or much later, or at the end of her life, is trying to tell the truth. No vagueness appears in what she says. We want to hear it, and the tone so far establishes her as a credible witness, at least to her own life. Why is this? First, she acknowledges her own guilt in not being available to her brother at his death, no matter how unexpected. She does not seize the obvious excuse that she didn't know what was happening, but she doesn't flog herself either. It was balanced. Going forward, we expect that she will say what things she never understood, that she would later take to the grave herself, since any possibility of resolution lies in the past. Properly constructed, the writer, and especially, the reader, will find a resolution for her that lies in the future. It will be the surprise that ties everything together and ends the book on a satisfying note. The door to this has been opened in paragraph one.

The risk of the First Person POV is that the teller of his story does not quickly capture our sympathy and identification. Check this carefully on the opening page, because the narrator should be clear, sympathetic, and identifiable in the first paragraph. This doesn't mean he knows everything, but his style of narration must create in the reader a strong desire to know his story. He must also evoke our trust, which is the belief that he will tell it as he really sees it.

I recently read one of Grahame Greene's spy novels in which the problem is finding the traitor in the midst of a group of agents at MI5. It's told in the First Person POV by one of the agents. I should say that I'm a big fan of most of Greene's work. However, at the end of the book it is revealed that the traitor is the first person narrator himself.

I felt betrayed. As a reader I had trusted the author to tell me the truth, once I was inside his head, as he had in many other books. I thought I was witnessing the story unfold without reservation and that the only things he did not tell me were those not relevant to the story. Maybe this book is a commentary on trust and its potential abuse, but all the same, I thought this was a grave error on the part of Greene. I was the reader, and not a character in the book that needed to be deceived to advance the story. It made me feel that the writer had been dishonest, and that is not the kind of game to play with your reader.

This is not to say the first person narrator may not himself be misled, naïve, misinformed, a victim or a failed observer about key facts in the narrative. Those can all be part of the fun. But the reader ought to be able to sort this out over the course of the action through clues and foreshadowing. What

I thought was dishonest was Green's narrator going around investigating his coworkers, considering for my benefit the pros and cons of evidence against them while at the same time he knew they were all innocent. I walked away feeling tricked, and here again is the rule that you should not disrespect your reader.

One of the interesting features of the First Person POV is the limit on what the narrator is able to know. He can only relate the events he has observed first hand or been told about. I chose in my mysteries to have the detective, Paul Zacher, be the first person narrator of the entire series. He has an ironic sense of humor, and how he interacts with events is best shown through his own impressions and the way he phrases his thoughts. He is a sentient person, and although a painter, he's still able to articulate his thoughts to the reader with a kind of tilted clarity.

The limitation that arises from this is that occasionally the reader needs to know information that Paul Zacher doesn't know himself. The solution I came up with is to use a few chapters in each of these books that are headed, instead of simply CHAPTER 5, with CHAPTER 5 and a character's name below it in block capitals. This chapter is then told third person from the exclusive POV of that character.

The chapter that follows resumes with the normal First Person Paul Zacher POV. This satisfies our rule of clarity, and if any reader has ever been put off by this system, I have yet to hear about it.

But wait, doesn't this mean that some characters may know more than the narrator, and the reader does too? What does that do to suspense in a mystery, or in any novel where the reader is trying to figure out what's about to happen?

This is a valid point, which is why I am always selective about what's revealed. It's enough to advance the structure of the story without giving away the end or identifying the criminal. If it does sometimes put the reader enough ahead of Paul Zacher that she may find herself saying to him, "Don't open that door!" that's OK. A mystery novel contains many such metaphorical doors, and she will never know what's behind all of them.

The advantage of First Person POV is that the reader can witness the character's development first hand as the story progresses. It has an intimacy that other POVs do not. Haven't you, in life, often wanted to look inside someone's head? While this POV will not always tell you what is really going on, it will tell you what that person *thinks* is going on. Even though it requires more of the writer to make the narrator character convincing and sympathetic, it pays off for the reader.

Another interesting and experimental book that illustrates the kind of risks writers can take is Elizabeth Kostova's *The Historian*. Here the narrative is First Person POV, but from two different people, father and daughter, a generation apart in the tale they're telling. It's handled so well that I was never once confused by who was talking. This is her first and extremely ambitious novel. Even so, I would never recommend a gamble of this magnitude for a first time novelist. Kostova is fearless.

Additionally, she has avoided the appearance of a series of flashbacks within this structure by making both narratives forceful and of equal weight and interest, even though they take place abut twenty years apart.

Clearly, POV is a minefield, where the most survivable route is the one you have thought through in advance. Start your characters, particularly the narrators, talking in your mind, and listen to their voices. Select the one that speaks to you most intimately, and with the greatest eloquence.

In a general way, the best POV for you is the one that makes you most comfortable and that advances your story in a natural fashion. Whatever it may be, make sure that as a writer in the early stages of development, you do not attempt something far beyond your skills. Always take chances, but take them in small doses at first. The magnitude of your chances should be such that you can learn from their lack of success without being damaged or derailed by it when it happens. Simple and consistent is definitely best no matter which POV you choose.

13.

ROMANCE

Romance (the emotional intoxication shared by two people, not the fiction genre) is a phenomenon most of us experience more than once, and it will find a place in nearly every kind of fiction and many kinds of nonfiction, such as campaign biographies. But while you will find chemistry in romance, you will not find romance in chemistry.

Recently I was given a copy of a new thriller that included an affair between the main character and a nightclub singer. On the cover it was billed as torrid. Of course, a good publicist will describe boiling water as *torrid*. The lovers' situation reminded me of a relationship I'd written about in one of my own mysteries, *Daddy's Girl*. Yet the encounters between them in this new book were as wooden and featureless as a conversation between two stones. They struck me as nearly phatic, with so little content in the phrasing that it felt like a script with no feeling.

These characters were the usual kind of

145

stereotypes we saw above. The man was dashing and handsome, engaged in a dangerous international job, the woman an exotic and gorgeous entertainer. The only possible reason they had for attracting each other was that we had been told they were *attractive*. The behavior of neither demonstrated any attractiveness for the reader. Their conversation was dull and composed of nothing but clichés. They were both inaccessible—there was no one present on the page. I set the book aside, utterly unmoved in scenes where I should've been deeply moved. They were no more than two manikins fumbling with each other's buttons and zippers.

While romance is a special effect between characters, and has its unique tone, it does not require a special kind of language or writing style. What *is* required is not to treat it as if it were occurring in some fourth dimension, where the diction is warped and twisted, and all other writing skills are discarded. The emotional tone of conversations between two people in a romantic situation possesses many of the same components as between two people who are angry, encouraging, skeptical, or nearly any other emotional context. Its romantic meaning will be conveyed by word choice, body language, and the ways you present the sensual ambience of the scene you've set.

The great volume of feeling between two people in love or in lust does not dispense with the need for skillful narration. In short, the emotions do not carry themselves; just because you say so does not make this a lofty moment. You as the author still need to make it work without telling the reader directly how to react to it.

The risk is that by treating the initial encounters that lead to romance as somehow fated or having a "special" aura, we finish by making them only artificial. Few romances have such remarkable and prescient beginnings. Let me give an example.

The evening I met my wife I was sitting in what used to be called a fern bar in a Victorian neighborhood in St. Paul. Our meeting had been arranged, although I didn't know what she looked like, and I was scanning women for likely candidates as they came and went. Sitting at a small, white, marble-topped table, I occasionally looked at my watch, not realizing that she didn't know her way around St. Paul, where I had lived for twenty-four years.

The entry I was watching was composed of two sets of oak double doors with the upper half glazed, a common way of attempting to keep winter at bay in Minnesota. The time was mid July, and the temperature was nearly 100°. Suddenly a commotion broke out in the small space between the paired doors, and I looked up to see a younger woman apparently throwing an elderly woman to the floor. Twenty-three months later we were married.

This misunderstanding of what I had seen was the start of a pleasant evening. It became a joke that opened our conversation, our first shared experience. The older woman had stumbled as she nearly fainted from the heat as she came in, and was being supported by the woman I was there to meet.

If you ask married couples how they got acquainted you'll get a wide range of stories, few of which have any overtones of fate or karma, and usually no ringing of bells or the subtle descent of fairy dust at the first encounter. Often the connection between two people hangs on some telling initial detail, and only expands afterward into a romance. The writer's task is to find that detail, because it humanizes the relationship and prevents what follows from being based on something as vague and clichéd as two people simply finding each other attractive because they're both model material.

For me, glimpsing my future wife for the first time as she was apparently beating up an old lady kept it from ever becoming a cliché.

In the relationship I drew in *Daddy's Girl*, detective Paul Zacher is shattered by the departure of his live-in girlfriend Maya. He ends up, some time later, connecting with a quirky Colombian nightclub singer named Yasmin Montoya. They begin a sexual relationship almost immediately, and Zacher finds himself wondering how to understand it. Here he's ruminating on the following morning about their first night together:

I kept going over our mutual seduction in my mind. The detail was exquisite, but the total experience seemed less than the sum of its parts. Scrambling some eggs, I finally dismissed these thoughts as unfair to her. Yasmin was right at the top of the babe scale, but it's possible I was expecting too much. She didn't owe me anything, and in the end, she would connect with me in her own way. Despite several near misses with Barbara Watt, I hadn't slept with anyone but Maya in six years and I had forgotten how different from each other women can be in bed, as well as in every other way.

Nothing lofty or frilly about that. What I wanted to accomplish in this relationship was to invert the old-fashioned theme of the girl playing hard to get. In this situation Yasmin Montoya is totally available to Paul Zacher sexually, but in no other way. I don't see her as at all immoral, since as a singer, she is constantly moving from town to town, and although she grows to like him enormously, she still can't make a commitment to any man. Paul, on the other hand, is looking to replace Maya with a solid emotional connection. He expects it to develop, and when it doesn't, he's distressed and mystified. Yasmin would prefer him to simply settle down and enjoy their time together, without always fretting about permanence.

You will recognize the potential in this for misunderstanding in dialog. Paul feels he's inching toward a deepening understanding as time passes, but Yasmin is already at the full distance she's willing to go. It lasts only a few weeks before she's gone.

This is an unusual pattern in a romance, but it illustrates one of many possible ways to bring freshness and drama to a subject as old as humanity. The Ken and Barbie doll situation I saw in the first book I mentioned offers no conflict, no development, and no interest.

As in many other aspects of creating a story, it is embracing the detailed and the particular that brings

the action and the emotional climate into focus.
Romance needs to lead to a crescendo of emotion,
but it's often so airbrushed and filmy that it comes off
as more bland than the rest of the story that enfolds
it. Keep it specific and make it real. It's OK if your
lovers fumble with the buttons.

14.

REVISION

Some writers would prefer to give birth to quadruplets simultaneously rather than revise their work. As if wearing blinders, others will bang out an entire manuscript before looking back at a single word. They are petrified of finishing the first draft for the same reason, and this invites a failure of closure. I'm not sure this attitude is helpful, since revision can be a primary tool almost from the first word.

To me, writing *is* revision—and that is the first definition I've attempted. It's an ongoing process that keeps me in touch with what I've already written and maintains it all aligned in the same direction. Think of the behavior of iron filings in the presence of a magnet. Usually when I sit down to work I first read what I wrote the day before. In this process I also strengthen the construction, supply any omitted words, and correct the spelling and punctuation. Does the voice ring true to both the narrator and the characterization? When I'm finished with this walkthrough, I'm in a position to supply the next sentence, because the first word of today comes directly from the last word of yesterday's work. Indeed, if you don't know how to get started, looking back in this fashion can point the way.

Part of this is about serendipity. On my first two books, I chose not to outline the plot, but to do a synopsis of it that I kept moving about five chapters ahead of where I was. Naturally, I already knew the ending. This was useful, but I soon discovered I could as easily keep that going in my head without writing it down. By maintaining the structure more loosely, I found I could allow for the introduction of elements and actions I hadn't anticipated, but that still flowed naturally from the position of the characters at any point. Even if you fear that this kind of serendipity will appear to be an absence of control, it still often happens that if you've developed your characters as living people on the page, they will take over and act on their own, sometimes surprising you. Contrary to the statements of writing coaches who advocate working from a formula, this is desirable. To be a working writer means that all of your abilities are working, not only the most superficial ones. Your mind is working at three levels: conscious, subconscious and unconscious, and times arrive when you let each of them go their own way. In fact, you have far less control over any of them than you might imagine. Their blended flow is the material good writing is made from.

Other writers work from a stack of note cards. They sketch out the high points of a scene on each one and pile them up. This is almost like the storyboard process in film writing, but without the illustration. It's not an approach I favor for myself, but it works for many writers who feel they can shuffle the cards about for different kinds of dramatic impact. Another potential benefit is that shuffling the scene order can reveal new ideas and outcomes. The writer sees possibilities his original sequential structural concept didn't suggest.

While there's no doubt that changes in sequence can influence the dramatic effect, the risk is that continuity and causality can suffer. There is also the danger of ending up filling in some of the narration as flashbacks, a kind of writing that inevitably slows the action and should be avoided when possible.

The reader will have realized several chapters back that a spontaneous character exists in my work. For a writer who was blocked for thirty-seven years, as I was, you might think that a careful and rigidly controlled process was the way back in. Don't take any chances now that you've got it back, right? For reasons I can't explain, the opposite was true. Once I started writing again, I learned early on to trust my process, of all things, the same one that had kept me locked in a closet for nearly four decades. Just as I don't question that process, I also don't ask why I trust it. There are times when you need to let the flow take over. If it works for you, autopilot is good.

If the next good idea remains out of reach, I go back and revise as a way of staying engaged. If it doesn't come at that moment, I still know that it will. If not everything makes sense at a rational level, some things may still work intuitively.

Revision includes a variety of approaches, and not all of them need to be massive and thorough. If you have a tendency to use certain words excessively, make them a target of one of your walkthroughs. In my case, I overuse the word *just*, among others. Most of the time it's a filler word and can easily be eliminated with no loss of meaning. I find that filler words, those that add little of substance to a sentence, are the ones most likely to be overused. A scan of your manuscript and a computer word search will tell you which ones bedevil *your* work. Another word to take a hard look at is *very*, one that adds nothing that a stronger adjective can't do better. I've almost entirely eliminated it from my work, although I occasionally allow it in dialog, where the speaker isn't working as hard to find a more precise word as I am.

Another weakness to watch for is the construction that begins with *there is* or *there are*. These phrases have a neutral quality that feels weak. While I rarely use them, I've never been successful in eliminating them completely, but substituting a stronger sentence opening is always desirable.

Adverbs should be another target of self-editing. Many writing coaches suggest they be avoided, but they constitute one of the seven parts of speech, and they can lend nuance to a sentence that is not always available with your verb alone. The problem comes from their frequent misuse. Whenever you use an adverb in your work, take a hard look at the verb it's coupled with. Can another verb be chosen that is stronger, and does not, therefore, depend on the amplification provided by the adverb in order to make your point? Do this substitution whenever possible. But when only the perfect adverb will do, and the verb is the best choice you can come up with after a serious effort, then use the adverb without hesitation. It is a legitimate writing tool, and if you use it correctly, you need apologize to no one.

The discipline of Rhetoric offers endless information about sentence structure, more than I ever dreamed was available. I own a filmed college course, one of the Great Courses series, that offers twenty-four half-hour sessions on the subject. For our purposes, much of it can be boiled down to the idea of variety. I make it a rule to not structure three consecutive sentences in the same way. He went here. . He went there…He went on without inspiration. Yet, repetition can play a role in achieving certain effects of emphasis, for example, setting up a series of parallel phrases, one of which does not belong. Make sure you use it consciously.

Vary your sentences in length and structure. The repetition of the same pattern puts the reader to sleep. Often it can be as simple as reversing the order of two clauses, although it goes well beyond that. Jack needed a jug of milk, so he went to the store. Needing a jug of milk, Jack went to the store. Long, complex sentences, a form that fans of Hemingway tend to be quick to condemn, can be rich in meaning, full of grace and elegance, lending nuance and subtlety to your narrative. You have just read an example.

Short sentences deliver punch.

This is also an example. It can easily stand alone in its own paragraph, which gives it additional emphasis. When the action is rushing forward, short sentences further accelerate the pace. It's almost like the effect of breathing hard. Combinations of long and short offer interest and variety. The flow of your paragraph is best developed not by traveling in a straight line, but by the twists and turns of navigating uneven terrain. I have said before that the best sentence in a chapter should be the opening one, particularly in the first lines of your book. Hook the reader, or she'll pull the next book in the row off the shelf and put yours back. You have at most one paragraph to seize and hold her attention, so you should operate as if you have less.

Another valuable scan is to check the strength of your verbs, aside from the adverb issue. Although this can invite beautiful writing, which I don't mind doing if it doesn't make me sweat, many verbs that may have been chosen in the rush of setting a series of sentences down on the page don't hold up well during a second, less hurried and more critical, scrutiny. They often bear the ordinary look of an easy first choice, words grabbed off the shelf on the run, as if the word store was about to close and you had to leave with something, *anything*. They lack the pointed quality of a more exact selection. I make it a practice to not employ a word that I know I'll have to change later. If you've used *went*, for example, think how many other, more graphic words might describe a passage from one place to another. If you're uncertain, one way to measure how well your verbs work is to ask how visual they are. A thoughtfully chosen verb evokes an image, and the more detailed and specific the image, the more power and precision your sentence has. Read verbs aloud in the context of their sentence and notice what visuals come to mind. If nothing does, then you need to do better.

Fiction succeeds partly on the strength of its specificity. We are not writing about changes in the monthly temperature range in Death Valley on a year over year basis, nor are we concerned with calculating the statistical likelihood of getting cancer if you smoked as a young teen. We don't want to know about groups or statistics as such. While our story concerns a group of individuals, it deals with them only as *individuals*, not as that group. The detail of a lock of hair on a woman's forehead lifting in the breeze—perhaps exposing roots of a different color; the matchbook left behind beneath a restaurant table as a way of propping up a short fourth leg; the word at which an incomplete sentence stops in a conversation as if at a roadblock. All these specific images bring the reader in for a closer look; they give her pause as they invite her attention. Some of your revision efforts should be directed toward expanding the punch and drama of your language in these situations, nouns as well as verbs, and making sure your pages are detailed and in sharp focus. It should require a mouse crawling up her ankle to give your reader a reason to look away from the page.

Even though I am primarily a fiction writer, I also do regular feature magazine articles and blogs. I bring the same approach to these nonfiction pieces. They are always narrative in nature, and full of detail and movement. They are never merely expository. As the author, I am usually present at the periphery of the story. Don't be afraid to use yourself in this way; you will never have a character you know better.

I've noticed a tendency among some writers to measure their progress by the number of words they write in a session, or in a day. The implicit goal is to make their manuscript bigger. But is a bigger manuscript better? Only if the quality of the words is equal to their volume. I see postings on Facebook all the time by writers who have set themselves a goal today of adding 2500 words, and they're pleased to be two-thirds there. Writing is not a task to be gotten through, and if the writer sees it that way, the reader will too. Never once have I seen these postings talk about what these words were. I'd like to see some excerpts from this kind of output. I can understand the need for this kind of thinking if productivity and writing discipline is a problem, but I don't recommend it for reasons I'll explain.

Contests exist with the goal of writing a novel in thirty days. All I can see from this is horrible and thoughtless composition. Writing and racing have nothing in common beyond their last three letters.

One risk in placing a premium on the quantity of output is that we tend to let this need for expansion creep into our sentences. They grow bulky in response, as if force-fed. Seven-word sentences grow to ten, twelve to sixteen. Superfluous adverbs and adjectives sprout like warts on a toad. We should properly ask at the end of a session, how much was the book improved by what we just wrote? Not how much did it grow. Quantity doesn't matter. Our manuscript will have as its optimum length the exact number of words it takes to tell the story best, and this number cannot be predetermined. You will recognize it only when you see it. It may also lie between you and your editor.

Cutting these extra words out, however, feels

too much like surgery. It's painful, and no anesthetic has been developed for overly voluminous writers in need of a gastric bypass. Worse, the outcome is that your manuscript finishes smaller than when you started this trimming process. For all of us who are building books, this is a horrifying prospect.

Yet, it has to be done, and it is done best by you. The key is to develop an eye for padded sentences, so that when we encounter one, it reads like a roadblock, which it is, one that must be removed in order to go on.

I'm going to take some examples of sentences that need surgery from one of my own unpublished books, titled, *The Disco Palace*. It's the sequel to a published thriller called *The Devil's Workshop*. At this writing, it's still in manuscript at 73,000 words and I've never been happy with the ending, although it contains elements I'm proud of. I'm leafing through it to find the kinds of padding I'm talking about, and I'll make these corrections in the manuscript as I go. Let's start with this line from the fourth page, where the character is inching along underground:

After a distance she couldn't measure, she saw light touching the edges of the stones surrounding her.

Here comes the scalpel:

After a distance she couldn't measure, light edged the stones around her.

The seventeen-word sentence goes to twelve. The missing words were unneeded. No other character had yet entered the book at that point, so the one seeing the light could only be the woman in question. The sentence is tighter and the verb more vivid. The goal is not to shorten the book, but to delete words that do nothing but pad the narrative. You will find that your pace improves by making changes like this. Look at these deletions as unwanted baggage you're forcing the reader to carry.

Here's another:

But she was still hopeful; there was a constant stream of candidates coming forward who failed to meet her standards.

With a few cuts and substitutions:

She was still hopeful; a constant stream of candidates advanced only to fail her standards.

Notice again that the verbs are strengthened and the sentence has more point with five fewer words. The rest was padding. I have mentioned earlier the there was construction. It's always weak, and now, in this sentence, it's gone.

He was searching for Rebecca, but he had few investigative skills that weren't operated by keyboard.

Here is the trimmed version.

Searching for Rebecca, he had no investigative skills away from the computer keyboard.

Beginning here with a gerund, we achieve sentence structure variation, too. You see the point of these examples, but why would I use extracts from my own work to show you padded prose? *Because I do it too.* I need to be constantly vigilant to eliminate extra words. I used this example because I hadn't looked at this manuscript in nearly two years, and I was less critical of my own work when I wrote this. In these examples you can see my bad habits, my way of stretching out sentences without thinking about it. Your path toward verbal obesity may be different, but spend some time examining individual phrases in your work for padding. If you overuse *seems like*, as I often do, try using a strong verb in its place. Most events do not seem like, they *are*. Use *seems like* to describe an actual illusion, or when you need a loose kind of simile to express an appearance that contradicts the reality beneath.

Be ruthless with yourself. Too many writers are self-indulgent, and their readers can often spot it before they do. If you can locate murderers hiding inside your head to bring into your fiction, you ought to be able to find extra words in your sentences. After all, it's a lesser offense, but one still punishable by reader impatience.

And now, the devil incarnate: proofreading, the final revision.

It is no secret that the more you look at a text error without recognizing it, the less likely it is that you will ever see it. Your always-helpful brain is fixing these problems for your eye unasked. If you have walked through your book five times, making corrections, checking verbs for strength and adverbs for a reason to exist on your page, searching for omitted words and scanning for spelling errors, the likelihood that you are now going to spot an error of spelling or a word omission is virtually nil. Yet, you know that a few must still persist.

Some programs, like Microsoft Word, have an editing function that is mostly concerned with targeting your phrasing and diction. This can be useful, but not life-changing, as many of the issues raised will be questionable in the context of your own writing style. Sometimes they flag the passive voice automatically, but you may still want to use it for specific situations. In this respect, this function can resemble a human editor, where disputes will arise about the appropriateness of some of your choices. Using a real editor, listen carefully to what you are paying for, but do not surrender your soul.

Another helpful aid, if your computer has this function, is to have it read the book back to you a half page at a time. Don't do it in segments larger than that because you need to focus on the words themselves without mentally drifting off savoring the delightful prose. This takes some effort, but it's worthwhile. What I like about it is that I can hear the absence of my skipped words, which my spellcheck will not detect. It will also flag the awkward grammar that may look plausible on the page but stumbles in the ear. I follow this with proofreading by a couple of friends who have a critical eye. It helps that they have not seen the manuscript before—they have hardly ever overlooked my errors, but it still can happen.

After all of this, I don't believe I have ever produced a flawless manuscript. Even if you hire a line editor, you are still not likely to get it, and the New York houses, who can afford to pay for six or seven proofreads, still don't catch everything, although they do better than I do.

15.

PROLOG OR NOT?

This is a controversial subject, and I'm going to come down on the less popular side of the debate.

Many writing coaches and instructors feel it's a mistake not to open directly with chapter one. The argument usually offered is that not doing so delays the story's initial action, and it is desirable to get the reader into the story from the first sentence. We already know that first sentences are *always* critical.

I don't disagree with the logic of this, but I want to suggest that a blanket avoidance of prologs eliminates some valuable tools. I use them myself in a little more than half my books.

I have said earlier that my mysteries are all narrated in the first person, so it's natural for me to look for ways of getting information to the reader that my narrator cannot know. Often this will take the form of focusing on an incident that in the story is only speculated about or referred to. This puts the reader in the position of knowing a piece of background that the principal characters never find out. This does the writer no harm, since every reader likes to be a little bit ahead of the game.

For example, in the second of my mysteries, *The Fifth Codex*, a fifth Mayan text comes to light. Its value is immense, and its existence had never been dreamed of. Its message, although 475 years old, has important political implications today among the Zapatistas in Chiapas. The prolog of this book shows a young boy concealing himself and then robbing the house in México City of an elderly woman who is being taken away to a rest home. The fifth codex has been forgotten in a sixteenth century trunk that is subsequently fenced to an antiques dealer in México City. He considers the codex to be a copy, and sells it for less than $500. It is then offered for resale privately in San Miguel, and this appearance is where the story moves to chapter one. Here is the opening paragraph of the prolog:

There are more than a few reasons to visit the Plaza San Jacinto in México City. Certainly one is the Bazar Sabado, where local artists come to display their work. There are also several reasons not to. One of these would have to be Pepe Perez, who was as fast as any kid in the San Angel neighborhood. At fifteen, he was slender and attractive; his dark hair lapped his ears and the dimples in his cheeks made him popular with girls. But even better, he could spot a business opportunity from a kilometer away, or even no more than arm's length, at the tips of his nimble fingers.

The young thief is not seen again in the main body of the book, but it is the codex that is the main character of the prolog. It is the hinge pin of the story that follows, and Pepe Perez launches its debut. Quite literally, the plot "turns" on it. One feature I insist on for my own prologs is that the action moves at least as quickly as it does in the rest of the book. Two paragraphs later, Pepe is inside the house watching the elderly woman being taken away by ambulance. Faster is better, so the prolog has that requirement of providing a compelling first sentence and a distinctive plot line. It relates directly to the coming action, and even though that action in the body of the book may do no more than refer to the plot segment we witnessed in the prolog, it becomes for the reader a compelling launch of the narrative and a beginning to the thread that continues through the entire book.

These prologs do not generalize the setting,

nor are they far removed from the central action, like some airy set piece that sets up the landscape of the book in broad pastel strokes. Quite the contrary: they are specific, detailed, and fast paced. Imagine a book that starts with a prolog describing the creation of the world and gradually moves toward a specific day and time. I have seen this done. The reader would be asleep long before the appearance of Noah and his ark.

I just glanced at a copy of James Michener's *Iberia*. It begins with a 37-page introduction. No one who is not an established writer could ever get away with this, and often it would still be cut or restructured by the editor, and it should be. But best-selling authors can get away with a great deal that the rest of us can't.

In the third of my mysteries, *Brushwork*, one of the principal characters had once been a touring Baptist preacher playing tent revival meetings that featured baptisms. During one such meeting, as he stood in the overflow water next to the cattle trough, a short in his microphone caused him to be electrocuted. A person in the crowd revived him and the scene quickly took on the legend that he had risen from the dead. Here's the prolog's opening line:

Malcolm Brendel had always known he was special, but he didn't realize how special until he rose from the dead at the age of thirty-three.

As an opening line, it's a grabber. The prolog illustrates this startling scene, even though it took place more than thirty years before the action of the book. But this early episode fueled the career of the character, and he is still trading on this glory as the action begins in chapter one.

My sense of the key issue for coaches who feel that prologs should never be used is that they often lack action. In the hands of the novice, they can act like a panorama of scenery unrolling at the back of the stage, setting up the story in a broad context, or they can feel like a flashback that interrupts the plot even before it begins to move.

In a way, the advice to eliminate prologs reminds me of the adverb use prohibition: it is based on the expectation of misuse. Understanding what that potential misuse means, and avoiding it, opens the door to including a prolog when you feel it has a necessary function. If you can make it work and it has the proper pace and freshness, trust your own instincts over someone else's rules that can often act as a way of denying you an opportunity you need.

You are the writer and the artist. Like a traffic intersection in México, creativity is a process where most of the rules are advisory in nature. Feel your way toward your own answer.

16.

EPILOGS

Why does the reader need an epilog if every angle and twist of the plot is already worked out and settled? Shouldn't the author have already wrapped it all up to the reader's satisfaction? Or is it only a way of applying a band aid to a sinking ship that should never have been launched without further work?

I can see that point of view. Of course everything of direct consequence to the action has been wrapped up. If some elements that were raised in the story went unresolved, a better approach would be to go back and remove them. After all, they couldn't have played any significant role. It is not the purpose of an epilog to explain what was not dealt with in the body of the text, but should have been.

I can recall how at the end of the movie, *American Graffiti*, the screen scrolled down with vignettes describing what happened later in life to the teenage characters. I felt it was a satisfying touch, and I regard the function of the fiction epilog in that same way. It was there as an extension, as if to say, "If you liked these characters, you might want to also know this about them." I can hear the purists now objecting. Perhaps rightly so, but we can sometimes indulge the reader and have fun at the same time.

Maybe it's the journalist in me that likes to walk away into the sunset, like Walter Cronkite used to do, saying, "And that's the way it is," with such authority. That was his epilog to the news of the day. But in doing that you do need to have told how it *really* was in the body of the text. Is it a need for closure of a kind that the tidy defeat of the villain, and the eager retreat of my Paul Zacher Agency into the cool confines of Harry's Bar in San Miguel, does not in itself fully provide? Perhaps. Or it may only be the luxury of kicking back after winning the game against a tough opponent.

The prejudice I grew up with is that after a long day's work you go home and unwind. You put your tools away; for example, Cody's handcuffs and lock picks. You clean your revolver and put on your comfortable shoes, and you reflect a bit on what worked and what didn't. Maybe it was too close a call and the Paul Zacher Agency was saved only by luck—an uncomfortable position to acknowledge. After all, the next case is coming in at some point, and it would be useful to know how to improve your process. To fail to grow in the detective business is to increase your unnecessary risk. This is true in almost any field of endeavor, but when we speak of risk taking in writing, we mean the kind that stretches our skills without risk of bodily harm.

In two books, *The Fifth Codex* and *The Book Doctor*, I used an epilog to show a newspaper report that gave an "official" version of what happened in the story. Both were wildly inaccurate. They give the reader the sense of being an insider witness to events that had been spun later by the press or the government. In doing this, they can also provide a little social commentary, something I don't mind doing now and then.

In *Brushwork*, I used an epilog to report a piece of correspondence from a person thought to have been murdered in the book. It's another ironic bit of fun. In *Daddy's Girl*, I showed the reunion of two characters that had been separated, an event not essential to the story, but vital to my readers who had been reading the series and were invested in their relationship. In *Strike Zone*, I wrapped up a subplot that referred to an earlier book. In *Vanishing Act*, the epilog was devoted to a funeral; again, not a vital part of the plot, but an occasion to comment on some of the action.

Your book need not be a mystery to benefit from having an epilog. Did you have a thread going through the story that was not vital to its resolution but still relevant? The epilog is the place to tie it off as a matter of interest to those readers whose curiosity was piqued. It can also be used to subtly set up a planned sequel.

An epilog does not slow the pace of the action, because it's largely finished. The reader is free to skip it without regret if she doesn't care for appendages at the front or back of her book, but if she has enjoyed your story for reasons other than the pace, she'll probably enjoy the epilog too. It can also be a means of commenting on your book, subtly, and never in a didactic manner. If the epilog is a gloss that will improve your reader's experience, go ahead and use it. You are the scriptwriter and the director. You will always encounter people who are more in love with rules than an artist needs to be, and this is why we're artists rather than probation officers.

17.

CHOOSING A TITLE

Here's another venture into a highly subjective aspect of writing. Perhaps you had chosen the title before you started your book. This may be an advantage, but at the end you'll still want to consider whether it remains a good choice given the way the book has evolved. Or maybe the title came to you halfway through it. You will still want to check that it remains a good fit.

If you are in a position where you need to search for a title, tradition supplies a number of resources to take advantage of. In the past many fine titles came from the Bible, not because they were destined for religious books, but because, especially in the King James Version, much of the language is strong and elegant. Think of a title like Steinbeck's *East of Eden*. While not elaborate, it is alliterative, laden with overtones, and it's not a phrase you are likely to encounter in conversation. If you're not familiar with the exact quote it came from, it makes you want to look it up. There are many others to be found with a little digging. Another great resource lies in Shakespeare's plays and poetry. Mining both of these for titles is a little old fashioned now, but it can still work well.

I also recommend Dylan Thomas's poetry for a more contemporary resource. You can find his complete work online. Other poets can also be helpful. I adapted the two titles of my vampire books from a line in Theodore Roethke's Poem, *In a Dark Time*. These titles are, *And Dark My Desire* and *And Darker My Wrath*. Poetry in general can be a tremendous source for titles because of the elegance and force of the phrasing. Think of *From Here to Eternity*, a bestselling book by James Jones and a popular movie. He borrowed the title from a line in a poem by Rudyard Kipling. One feature all these titles have is that they are rarely found in ordinary conversation. This gives them a quality of resonance. You know you're hearing an unusual phrase. You will be most successful if you can find a chapter or passage in any of these sources that connects with the main theme of your book. If your subject is betrayal, for example, look into *Macbeth* or the thirty pieces of silver scene in the New Testament.

Failing that, the Internet can supply

websites full of book titles. They have a more random feel, and might therefore be less helpful. Also ask the test readers of your manuscript whether they have any suggestions. I've found that they have often thought of one, but might be hesitant to suggest a title change unless you ask. You can unearth people around you who love to be part of the literary scene, even if they're not writers themselves. They will read your works in progress, your "finished" manuscripts, and some will even proofread your work. Use them with sincere gratitude and give them credit on your acknowledgment page, because you will never find more loyal and supportive readers than these.

An agent once told me that he thought a successful title is no more than the title of a successful book. I tend to doubt this, since I think the title contributes to the success of the book in the same way the cover does. An arresting title gets a book pulled off the bookstore shelf faster than a dull one, and that's the first step toward getting it sold and read. Look at successful titles of some of the books you've read and ask yourself what it is about them that gives them resonance.

Robert Ludlum was a prolific writer who still puts out a lot of books despite the fact that he's been dead for more than ten years. I call that impressive momentum, although some readers are offended that other people are writing them under his name. His format was always the same. His titles were three words, invariably starting with the: *The Bourne Identity*, *The Matarese Circle*, *The Holcroft Covenant*, *The Parsifal Mosaic*. None of these are alliterative, but they still have an attractive resonance that stays with us. You want the reader to remember the title easily. They also sound somewhat exotic. You won't see one called *The Candy Bar*, or *The Boston Bean*; they are too ordinary. There is more to these titles than the three-word format. They are welcome to the ear in a way that more common phrases with the same rhythm are not. In the consideration of any title, you should say it aloud repeatedly and ask other people to say it to you.

My advisor at San Francisco State, Herbert Kubly, was a dashing man with a curl at his forehead and a cleft in his chin. He came from a town north of Madison, Wisconsin called New Glarus, a Swiss enclave where his family owned a large farm. "Nick" Kubly was a playwright at an early age, and one of his efforts was titled *Inherit the Wind*, also a phrase from the King James Bible. It was a great title. You are now saying to yourself, I didn't know Herbert Kubly wrote *that*. Well, in a way he did. He wrote his play in 1946, and it was produced on the London stage in 1948. It was successful, but it was not, however, the far more famous play of the same title about the Scopes Trial, which appeared in 1960, and went on to become a blockbuster movie.

The lesson is this, for us as well as Nick Kubly: book and play titles cannot be copyrighted. Anyone can take yours, and conversely, you can take anyone else's. Does this mean you should name your book, The Bible? After all, it's always sold pretty well; why not see if you can get some coattail action out of that? Or how about *The Da Vinci Code*? That was another hot item.

Perhaps you're too shy to copy one directly. How about not taking the exact title, but only coming close enough to suggest it? For example, how about *Fifty-one Shades of Grey*? Some readers might think your version has one more kinky twist than the original, or for people who can't remember the name of the author, maybe it could even pass itself off as the sequel.

Here we once again encounter that issue of respecting your reader, part of what in the next chapter we'll call the writer's ethic. She will feel deceived if she chooses to buy titles like these. But what if you come across a title that you really like, and it's already been used? Ethically, do any conditions exist that allow you to still use it?

Here's a close-to-home example. I knew before I started this book that I wanted to call it *A Writer's Notebook*. The text has an informal and personal tone. It's obviously not a textbook. I was writing about my experience of what works and what doesn't, but not putting myself forward as a guru. My thought processes and my starting points are hopefully quite clear. It charts the course of my learning process in writing. My first step in this title search was to look at Amazon and see if the title had been used before. I wouldn't have been surprised if it had, although I didn't expect the first entry to come up would be a 1949 book of the same title by one of my favorite authors, Somerset Maugham. His version was literally a notebook full of ideas, sketches, starts and stops, comments and short pieces. A useful book, and still available, but it is not like this book. The title comes up several other times, always followed by a different phrase for the subtitle, or out of print. On this basis, I saw no reason not to use it myself, especially with the unique subtitle, *Everything I Wish Someone Had Told Me When I Was Starting Out*. This alone set my book apart from the others. It makes it clear that this book is gleaned from my experience in the muddy trenches of learning to write, and it's aimed at people early or midway into the process who would like to avoid some of the mistakes I so innocently made. In some senses it's actually a preventive, since in reading it, you can discard my mistakes without making them yourself. I mentioned above that writers often write for themselves. This book is a perfect example, but for the timing, since I needed to be using it in 1964. Who was it that said timing is everything?

Here we encounter once again part of that idea that comes up in the next chapter. It's about ethics in writing, and your treatment of your reader as well as your peers. The bottom line on previously used titles is this: using the title of this book in no way trades on the reputation or the sales momentum of any of those other books. No one remembers Maugham's book sixty-plus years later, so no one can confuse mine with it. The book in your hands is not a copycat work. If I had been able to find anything like it, I would've bought it years ago, not bothered to write it, and saved myself a lot of grief. I could've gone on to write more fiction in the time I saved. Nothing either recent or selling in any volume has this title. Nor does any book in the writing category have this subtitle. My book will rise or fall on its own merits, based only on my ability to write it and promote it. And this is the bottom line—if you can say all these things about a title that has been already used, even more than once, one you'd like to use again, go ahead and use it without hesitation, but make sure the book inside those covers is your own.

18.

HANDLING THE TRUTH

Now your writing is launched. With the aid of the exercises, the page one anxiety is gone. Having absorbed the thoughts about revision, you're staying in touch with what you've already written, and from your plot map, you're confident of reaching your destination. Your process is there, no doubt about that, and if you don't analyze it too closely, it stays with you. Momentum has become part of your engagement, and it feels good. You recognize from the POV chapter that I'm now using the Second Person version on you again. To your delight, you've already discovered that the world of fiction can be marvelously inventive—you can simply make everything up, right?

Or can you?

A series of foul doubts climb like vermin on a rope ladder into your mind. What is your obligation to this story, now thirty-one pages long? Coherence, certainly, clarity of writing, and credibility in plot and character. A close focus on the kind of detail that brings it alive. You have already noticed one thing you didn't expect—that even though this story is fiction, it is still somehow true in a way you couldn't have defined before, a way you never expected, but you can still feel it. That truth resides in the way it hangs together, how the elements interconnect, the logic of their relationship. If you tapped this new structure with a mallet, even in its incomplete state, it would positively ring, because it has nothing faked or loose in its construction. It has no filler. Now you understand what people mean when they describe what they sensed was a false note in some other piece of fiction. Because of this realization, you have already begun to feel an obligation to your own burgeoning truth, and by implication, to yourself and your reader. You know you have to get the rest of it right, and that means there is a *right* to be gotten in order for it to be true.

Defining what that means is the beginning of the writer's ethic.

But when you attempt to determine what the truth means in this context, the truth you are now working with in your own book, one that contains the elements of your own soul as print, you draw a blank. It is not like what you are accustomed to thinking of as truth. Does this mean different kinds might coexist? How can that be, if truth is an absolute, a principle you grew up with, the touchstone against which other things are measured?

Jack Nicholson famously said to Tom Cruise in the 1992 movie *A Few Good Men*, "You can't handle the truth!" This line has a resonance that survives today—a remarkable feat for a statement that is fundamentally *untrue*, because at a personal level, no single ongoing truth exists to be handled.

The reality is that we all handle the truth every day—but it is only the truth of that day, not of yesterday or tomorrow.

Surely, you say, some things are dependably true, and we can gain access to them. For example, we can look up the meaning of words in the dictionary. But wait, the meaning of words changes over time. Many words signified different things coming from the pen of Shakespeare or Dickens than they do today. Others have disappeared entirely. When did you last call someone a cad or a bounder? You may know what these words mean, but you would never use them now. But that was fiction, so why not look at science, where information is generated from measurable facts. That must be true, and isn't it more comfortable? Maybe the truth can be found in those books included in the category of *nonfiction*—a term whose meaning, or at least, whose intent, is perfectly clear, a world of dependable facts at last.

Maybe, but as a writer of both fiction and nonfiction of some experience, I regard nonfiction as a subcategory of fiction. Its chief distinction is that it overtly proclaims itself to be "true." In some other senses, the differences are not as clear.

The truth of nonfiction is often the victim of time. If I want to learn chemistry it would not pay me to pick up a textbook from 1969, yet it was among the hardest of hard sciences when that book came out, and still is. That was the year humans landed on the moon for the first time, so they must have known something reliable. But the "truth" of chemistry has proven to be fluid, and although it's no less (or more) "true" than it was then, it's different today, and it will continue to evolve.

Similarly, the biography of George Washington on your bookshelf was written by someone who never met him, never heard him speak, and is based on information that is second, third or fourth hand. The gaps between the recorded facts of his life that the author has filled in are no more than merely *plausible*. If we know Washington did this, then we can be pretty sure he did that, right? Testimony of this kind would never be admissible in court. Much of the truth in nonfiction is no more than inference.

The nonofficial conversations attributed to Washington were rarely written down, although we can find them now in his biographies. Even during his lifetime his legend was being constructed, which naturally involves the selection of what details to use, which to omit, and which to embellish or construct from whole cloth. Yet, as biography, this is classed as nonfiction, even though we find it riddled with conjecture and "half-truths," a term most difficult to define. Is it like half-life?

You already know that the autobiography you are now working on in an attempt to preserve the "true" story of your life is full of omissions, too. Some are the casualties of faulty memory; others are conscious deletions you made because of embarrassment, or from the fear of provoking an unfavorable reaction from your family and friends. You realize you have gotten away unpunished with a number of shabby actions you don't care to admit to now, even though they weren't serious. Furthermore, the sheer limitations of space require the elimination of myriads of things you know about yourself but have no room to put down. Since you feel a responsibility to edit your own work before the real editor sees it, you have discarded them as unimportant. Other facts that may be meaningful to you were eliminated because you don't think the reader would be interested. In this spirit, you have already deleted three pages detailing your collection of the postage stamps of the minor Indian States in the nineteenth century. Yet, how can we trust your objectivity as you make these choices? You have also cut out ten thousand other things in order to examine fifty in detail. How can so fragmentary a picture of your life be *true*? If it were art, it might be inexpensively framed and sold as no more than a hasty sketch.

Of course, much of this cursory treatment is only because the material consists mainly of detail. Beyond and monolithic are the vitally important events you remember so clearly. Surely these events are true with a capital T, since you have never for a single moment forgotten them. They are the trustworthy landmarks of your life, and because they are the part of your memory that is carved in stone, they must be dependably true. If not, then what else is?

For example—and this, although you're not ready to write it yet, will figure prominently in your life story—you remember the time you had that terribly traumatic experience when you were eleven years old. You can see it in a frame frozen in time. Your reaction was immediate and devastating. Fully an hour went by before you could speak coherently. Naturally, that night you did not sleep, blaming yourself. In the morning, you felt marginally better, but you were exhausted. It was a week before you started to settle down, even though you couldn't get it out of your mind. You already knew that it would affect you for the rest of your life.

Two years later you are beginning to suspect it wasn't as big a deal as you first believed. You are able to talk about it to your closest friend, but never to your parents.

You are twenty-six years old before you realize quite suddenly that it wasn't really your fault, a hurdle you've never been able to leap. It was caused by the bullying adult—a friend of your parents—who immediately shifted the blame to you. Later, it is only when you have a child of the same age as you were when this event occurred, that you begin to take on a different and more mature perspective, one that has always eluded you in the past.

Now you are fifty-one years old. Your index finger is poised over the keyboard of your computer as you work on this autobiography, this reasoned retelling of your life story. You have reached the pivotal point in the book. From the sober base of your current maturity, you are now ready to sum up this episode, but you hesitate—what is the truth? Is it the way you felt at the moment of that event forty years ago? Is it the way you regard that moment now? Or is it somewhere between? And if your viewpoint now is the truth, why is today's now any better than the entire chain of daily perspectives you have evolved through during the years since it happened? Won't the now of today be invalidated by the now of tomorrow, just as yesterday's now is no longer true in the way that it was *then*?

This is sounding like the question asked of President Nixon during the Watergate crisis: "What did you know and when did you know it?" Inevitably it brings up your ethical awareness, since you have pledged to yourself to tell the "truth." My, this is much harder than you thought. Maybe it's easier to stick to fiction. Your face in the computer screen reflects a look of dismay.

Some years ago at a writer's conference I spoke with Rebecca Walker, who wrote an important and successful memoire titled *Black, White and Jewish*. I put this same problem to her, especially the long passage of time between a series of events and writing about them. She thought for a moment before responding. Then she said, "The truth can only be the way it looks as you write it."

Another time I sat down with filmmaker Caren Cross and her husband, Dave. With his help, she had made the film, *Lost and Found in Mexico*, several years earlier. We were having a conversation that became part of my book on the expat experience. I was talking about my own process of editing taped conversations, the process of deciding what was cut, what got corrected, and what made it into the book.

I sit there opposite the Crosses wondering about the same process writ large as the editors cut 120 hours of footage into fifty-three minutes of finished film. How could it make any sense? How could it resemble at all what people had said?

"I knew right away what was good," says Caren. "The cream rose to the top."

"But," I ask, "is the film true?" This is equivalent to asking if the three and a half years she spent on it was wasted. "Because it's been worked up and worked over and cut back and forth." My arms are making broad slashing motions. She probably thinks this is what I imagine film editing is like. It's done with a machete.

"I think it's absolutely honest. It's honest for me, so it's my truth."

In the term, "my truth," lies an interesting distinction between truth and honesty, and implicit in this statement is a kind of subjectivity that contradicts the set-in-stone quality we normally think that the truth possesses.

I believe the answer is that truth is a process composed of two elements. One is the fact or event that you experienced. It was over when it was over, and as time passes, it does not change in itself. The second component is your *reaction* to it, which began instantly and evolves continuously as you gain in years and experience, maturity and wisdom—in other words, the *memory* component. Memory is a warehouse with flexible walls. Every item you have stored inside it is in a state of constant flux. Because of that, the truth is literally a moving target, and since the second of the two elements that make it up is always in motion, the combination of these two has no stable content. It varies continuously with the passage of time, even though one element within does not change. So where do you turn for truth of a more dependable kind? Does anything have permanence? Is real credibility only a dream?

The answer, I'm afraid, is that you turn to fiction, a term often used as a synonym for a *lie*.

I have heard it said that truth is the exclusive domain of the fiction writer, because he cannot be contradicted. You are not able to say to me, even as you read my book that has parts you disagree with, or that may offend you, that I have not told the truth. You cannot read my mind, and since it is my obligation as a writer to tell the truth as I know it (on that day), your wiser course is to concede that I have. If I have succeeded well enough, which is to say that I've been persuasive and plausible, you can also recognize that fact, even as you perceive that my truth may differ from yours and still be valid.

The *truth* in fiction will possess the following characteristics: it will feel profound even when it's a statement or conclusion you've never thought of before. It will apply almost universally, so it will lack the kind of short-term specificity that is invalidated by the flux of changing events. It will transcend gender, race, age, politics, and nationality. Reading it will uplift you, and from that momentum, may even lead to other insights in unrelated areas. And most of all, it will have the kind of symmetry and simplicity that can only be described as beautiful.

The rest is only news and reminiscence.

19.

WRITING NONFICTION

I noted in the previous chapter that I regard nonfiction as a subcategory of fiction, the only one that seeks to bill itself overtly as the truth. It's interesting that this word, *nonfiction*, defines that category of writing in negative terms: nonfiction is *not* what fiction is. Why are we not told any more than that about what it is? Perhaps no better definition exists. I know that I don't have one. We've already looked at the reasons for considering it to be true or not, so I'm going to concern myself in this chapter with thinking about how nonfiction writing differs from fiction techniques.

When I began blogging for promotional reasons a couple of years ago, I found myself back in the realm of nonfiction. I had written my book on the expatriate experience earlier, but when it was finished I had no plans to write more. I was eager to get back to fiction.

My first blogs were about writing, especially

my experience of thirty-seven years of writer's block. This necessarily involved placing myself and my thought processes in the spotlight in a way I had not done in the expat book, where I was no more than a facilitator guiding the conversations, and a commentator mainly in the Introduction and Conclusions chapters. The character of the blog writing was suddenly much more personal, and I wasn't initially all that comfortable doing it. I had never felt the need to write an autobiography, since I believed that much of my life experience emerged in my fiction in a somewhat fermented form—just how I wanted it.

I quickly learned to accept myself as a character in these nonfiction pieces, as I realized that since much of what I was exploring had happened many years earlier, the revelations I made as I probed what must have been going on in my head didn't seem to hit that close to home.

This illustrates an important feature of nonfiction, which is that your characters will be based on people living now or who have lived in the past. Unlike the characters in fiction, where no one can contradict you, here you are open to a vast range of quibbles from your readers. One way to deal with this is to keep your real-life actors focused on the events specific to the story, and not try to develop them any more than they need to be—unless your book is a biography. Better to be criticized for omitting something a reader thought should be there, than guessing wrong as you flesh things out in unnecessarily broad and questionable strokes.

In this respect, much of nonfiction shares an approach with fiction. I'm assuming you are not doing a book based on statistics and trends, where generalization is the goal. I often see a tendency in writers of nonfiction to think that no special skills are required, and that because much of the material is factual and unembellished, it needs no strategy to involve the reader. As a longtime reader myself, I find this attitude insulting. Let me suggest that the reader of nonfiction is still in need of persuasion to read your book in preference to every other, and your technique lies at the core of that persuasive effort. Especially if you are doing a memoire, or travel writing, you will want to employ the same kind of telling detail that brings fiction to life. The process and effect will be no different. Use your sense of fine detail in describing the appearance and actions of your real-life characters.

An autobiography presents your life from an early age up to the time of writing. Memoirs embrace a much more limited period, your four years as an intern in the Clinton White House, for example. It will be a segment of time with an inclusive theme that brackets your story in ways that go beyond the fact that these events all happened to the writer. Naturally, you will not have the latitude for improvisation that fiction allows. Many of your telling details will have to be extracted through research. Your characters will not be able to take wing in the unlimited ways you might want. Nor will you be able to add layers of nuance as you can in fiction. You are constrained by facts, insofar as you can unearth them.

The principles of dialog, setting, pace, and plot that we've already discussed will not differ significantly with nonfiction. The methods of ending a chapter with suspense will still apply to your advantage. Nor will you require a different set of exercises to help get you started, if that's a problem. Your book will still be interesting mainly to the extent that you cast your story in a dramatic context, one you will have to generate by the way you structure the facts and events you know about your character's life. Learn how to hold things back and release them at the correct moment for maximum impact. Examine the writings of your subject for their emotional content and include this in your story. Learn to read documents for their subtext, a level of half-concealed information that is always present in written sources, as it is in the speech of all of us. Don't forget to leave some air in your text for the reader to fill. Your real-life character, whether it's you or not, will need to be on a compelling journey, one laden with obstacles than need to be overcome one by one on the way to a final triumph. While one real distinction between fiction and nonfiction is that nonfiction contains more information presented directly as such, the techniques of delivering the story in a compelling way are not fundamentally different.

Travel books work best when inhabited by real travelers, ones that are relatable, to use a word we've seen before. They are encumbered by real baggage, not all of which is handled by the porter. Every scene they take in is viewed through the lens of their own experience. Make your reader want to be in the railway coach next to them, or occupying the adjacent stateroom on the Rhone barge cruise. In this case, the trip is the plot, but it is either driven or impeded by the detail you provide. Include the great landmarks, like the Eiffel Tower, the Hagia Sophia, but only in passing. Everyone has seen a thousand photos of them, so focus on sights, sounds, and ambience the reader doesn't know or expect. Make it more than just scenic wallpaper. Show your characters engaged and active. Travel can cause anxiety and frustration, as well as excitement and exhilaration. Let's see these forces operating on your travelers. As in your fiction, the setting is a major actor too, full of mood, odors, sounds, and sights. Food and drink can be important players in these stories. Unless the plot includes considerable doubt about getting there, don't end your book with arriving home. It should finish on a high note in an exotic place, a crescendo. After she pauses to wonder why you would ever come back, the reader will be left wondering when your next book is coming out.

What I found works well in magazine articles and blogs is telling a story; it's nonfiction as narrative. I did a Mexconnect piece on an organization in San Miguel that builds free houses for desperate families in the countryside. Naturally some factual information was embedded in it, but it was framed as the director and I making a visit to a house in progress, and another one that was recently completed and occupied. The unspoken theme was transformation, where the lives of people with no hope of bettering themselves where changed almost overnight. I also included the director's progress from his role as the dean of adjunct faculty at a New York college, to bricklayer's helper in México, to president of the organization.

This type of narrative arc gives the reader a sense of movement and action. I know that my target reader is looking for a taste of what this kind of community engagement is like, not a list of all its attributes. If I have left you with the impression that my nonfiction looks a lot like my fiction, it does. I think it's risky to draw major lines between the two.

I have been known to ask among my writer friends whether they're certain that nonfiction actually exists. It is a question not every one of them is comfortable with.

PART TWO

THE BUSINESS OF PUBLISHING

20.

FINDING AN AGENT

Naturally, you will need an agent only if you are aimed at traditional publication in New York. I don't know of any of the old line publishers that will look at a manuscript anymore if it's submitted directly by the author. They rely on agents to screen out the unworthy and whip the accepted writers with potential into shape. Once accepted by the agency, your job is not done, because your new agent may demand anything from an edit to a complete rewrite.

It's not hard to imagine why successful agents are like Marilyn Monroe; everyone wants to have a close personal relationship with them. Obviously, their sanity depends on playing hard to get. As the author of a completed manuscript, you are now the suitor charged with the task of breaking through all the barriers between yourself and the perfect agent for your book.

The best resource for finding an agent is if you know a writer who has an agent he's happy with and is willing to recommend you. This implies that he thinks you would be a good fit for that agent's clientele, in other words, his contacts within the old-line publishing industry. This ought to at least get you a serious read.

After that, does your writer friend know an agent that handles books similar to yours, but he's not willing to recommend you (or anyone)? At least then you can submit your manuscript with a note that says you got his name from your writer friend.

Failing both of these options, you can start your research on the Internet. Many sites have lists of agents broken down by category. Agents tend to specialize. Focus on your field, from nonfiction or fiction, to which genre you write in. Avoid any agent who would charge you a fee to read your work, or has a fee structure thereafter. He should be marketing your book at his own expense, subject to reimbursement when it sells. This is only good incentive. His cut should be 15% of domestic royalties and perhaps a bit more abroad, when there is another agent acting as intermediary to a foreign press. Spend some time on the craft of writing a query letter. Many fine examples can be found online. Keep in mind that agents are busy and don't have time for queries that are not direct and to the point. Think of your query letter as a sample of your strongest and most concise writing. That's how it will be judged. If it's weak or self-indulgent your book will never see daylight.

Another way to select a list of agents to submit to is by looking at the acknowledgment page of writers who create the same kind of books you do. Many authors will thank their agent in this space. On Amazon, you can usually look at this page and then go to that agent's website. There are also sites where you can type in the writer's name and his agent's name will come up. It will save time to have prepared from your research a short list of agents who specialize in the kind of books you write. Before you send any query letters, check the Internet sites that evaluate agents for any comments. Search the words, *bad literary agents*. You will find many of them, and some can be predators.

When you start sending queries, set up a simple spreadsheet with the names and websites of the agents you have approached, along with the date. Don't try to keep track of it in your head. Most agents will not respond if they aren't interested, but they will offer a time frame within which you will hear from them if they are. Put the closing date of this period in too so you know when to write off a given agent. If you get a positive response, carefully study the agent's website for his rules for manuscript submission, particularly in the matter of format. Most agents will take email submissions in preference to paper manuscripts, and many will start with an excerpt, often the first thirty pages.

If you find some serious interest developing, ask who else that agent represents. How many book deals has he made? As in cover design and other aspects of self-publishing, this is no time to be working with a beginner. If he can't offer a reasonable track record, move on, because signing with him will only tie you up and waste your time.

If he offers you a contract take a careful look at it. Have a lawyer check it out. Does it, for example, prevent you from self-publishing if he hasn't sold the book within a set period of time? Try to anticipate what your obligations might be if a prolonged period passes with your book unsold. If you take it back, do you owe him anything? It's too easy to go into these deals thinking only of your desired outcome. You need to think about every contingency. Don't hesitate to contact, possibly through their websites, other authors represented by this agent. See whether they're satisfied. If they're not, that might make them more eager to talk to you. More than many others, this project is top heavy with research.

21.

PUBLISHING WITHOUT NEW YORK

To paraphrase a one-time presidential candidate, here's an inconvenient truth: In addition to being first a craft, and hopefully an art, writing is also a business. Without publishing and promotion, the business end of it, you might as well be addressing a wall, because you have no audience, and that inaccessible audience is the other half of a writer's world. When you touch your fingers to the glass before your eyes, it's the second set of fingertips that rises to meet yours on the other side.

The traditional publishing business model offered two options. The first involved finding an agent, whose job was to screen out those unworthy of being published, and pitch the remaining few to New York. If he sold your book, you were assigned an editor whom you worked with to put it into shape, which was not always the shape you had envisioned for it. Once the editing was complete, your book was consigned to the salesmen, whose task was to figure out how to sell it. Your title going in was *Romance Among the Petunias*. What the sales team came up with, after a tumultuous session, was *Sex Among the Slugs*. After looking at the sales figures of some other recent books, they wanted *gritty* where you had seen a kind of floral elegance blooming. They felt this was more incisive, more down to earth. Now you're afraid your mother-in-law will see it if she reads the book page in her hometown paper. This was never how you thought success would be.

Publishers also used to have what was called a "midlist," a collection of authors who were not well known but had potential. The idea was that the publisher was willing to spend a little time and money on startup for your writing career.

The midlist is largely gone now, a victim to financial reality, since the industry is under siege for falling behind the times. You will be able to sell a fiction manuscript to New York only if it fits the pattern of what they think will sell in mass quantities. The fact that this is your first book will be a big negative, because you have no track record to reassure them, and they already have other reasons to lie awake nights much larger than the one you're bringing them. A nonfiction manuscript will be just a little easier, and only then if it's accurately aimed at an identifiable niche audience. The barriers to you or anyone breaking through are now higher than ever, although it still happens.

After reaching that point, it used to be that you could go to what was called a vanity press and get the book published at your own expense. Offset printing was the only feasible option, and to obtain a reasonable unit cost you needed to order about 3,000 copies. Naturally, no distributor would handle it, so you had to schlep them around to bookstores yourself. Because your name meant nothing to anybody, no bookstore wanted you, so it was all uphill and tragically steep. Here's why in more detail, since even though your novel is wonderful, that has little bearing on your situation.

Suppose your book is an inch thick, a common size in trade paperbacks. The bookseller knows exactly what that inch of shelf space costs to maintain every month. This is, after all, a business to him and he has substantial rent, inventory, staff, health care costs and other overhead to cover. He may have his store in a state that taxes his inventory once a year, another incentive for him not to know you. The bank requires him to make payments of principal and interest on his operating loan every month. He has probably pledged his house equity as part of that financing package. While he would like to offer every book in print because he loves them, the only number he can afford to look at is how many times that inch of shelf space is emptied by a sale, refilled, and emptied again in the course of the next thirty days. He will have to balance the unknown sales potential of your book against the established track record of books by Michael Connelly or John Grisham. You are now beginning to grasp the economic side of the problem, which dominates this entire picture.

This is why three years later the remaining 2,971 copies of your book have gotten moldy from sitting untouched in your damp basement, and you have to pay someone with a pickup to haul them off to the dump. Why did no one tell you this in advance?

That is the publishing and retail distribution side of the picture, not the author's, so now let's retreat a step or two to the moment when you got your manuscript back from the editor and made those final changes, because it was at this point that you needed to start thinking differently about the publishing process. Let's examine the book world as it is today. You are aware of the new revolution in self-publishing in a general way, but like most starting writers, you still feel the need to be able to walk into your favorite bookstore and run your finger down the spine of your own novel. That's what makes it real, and even contemplating that moment gives you an almost indecent thrill. Naïve or not, let's say that you opt for the traditional New York way as your best shot at being able to do that.

So let's now assume you're ready to publish your great novel, the one that took you eight years of agony to write, but no one's interested. You even found an agent. Signing with her made you feel you were really on your way, but now she rarely returns your calls, and you don't know exactly what she's doing with your manuscript. You looked briefly again at self-publishing options, this time in more detail, but when you scanned the lists of self-published books on Amazon, your stomach became all fluttery, and you knew you could never be part of that pathetic loser crowd, because Your Book Is Different.

Every day you get up and you're a day older, but that's the only thing in your life that's truly in motion. When you attended an expensive writer's conference in a western city, you found that most of the other attendees were much like you; only their book was probably not as good, or in most cases not even finished. You felt superior to most of them because you already had a completed book and an agent, while they were no more than wannabes.

The reality is this: it's been a great run, but the old-line New York publishers are not what they were. Through bankruptcy and merger, their ranks have thinned. Although they position themselves as the gatekeepers of great writing, working to exclude the unworthy, they are mainly focused on a shrinking bottom line. They are in a distinctly defensive mode, and the unknown writer is one of the people they need to defend themselves against. They know that the business model is changing, and next year will be even tougher than this one. Who's next to go down? Their secret fear is that they will end up merging with another firm they have always thought of as bums, not even second-class. They are correct, because publishing technology has taken a left turn, while they continued in a straight line. After all, it worked so well in the past, why mess with success? Their favorite obscenity is *Amazon Kindle*. Reading this chapter is now giving you a headache.

Let's look at their product. The top two or three percent of the books they put out are excellent, top-quality work. The level below that, say about fifteen or twenty percent, are solid, workmanlike books that, although they may not be inspired, still deserve to find an audience.

The seventy-five to eighty percent below that

is of little interest, and often a waste of the paper it's printed on. Writers who have produced great books in the past are allowed to write self-indulgent drivel unchallenged. Others who sell well put their names on books they didn't write, even when they're dead. Look for the real author's name in small print at the bottom of the cover. The old-line publishers are no longer serving either the reading public or the writers who seek to inspire it. They can't remember when they last published anything that looked like a gamble. For the new writer trying to get through this no man's land, it's like navigating a logjam in a birch bark canoe—a chancy situation.

And here is one more obstacle. You can also be rejected because the publisher is looking for a certain kind of book, a focus that may not be obvious. He may be thinking he wants the next *Da Vinci Code*, or a new rehash of some other bestseller. If your book does not fit this narrow profile, it won't be considered, no matter how good it is.

Worse, the alternative is chaos—the self-publishing world, where 96% of the output is worthless. There is no barrier at all to publishing trash, but in self-publishing, at least you're sure to get your book out there, if you can pay the often modest—but not always—price of entry. But where's the appeal in that if there's no exclusivity? And to think you were raised to believe merit counted for something.

Still, there are some strong similarities between New York and this trackless wasteland. In both places you will do *all* your own marketing. That's right, all of it. The old line publishers spend their entire promotional budget on their top five or six best sellers. Get ready to dedicate 65% of your time to doing promotion, a task you know nothing about, other than that you suspect it's something successfully done mainly by people wearing bowties who can never tell the truth. The reality about writing is that the actual placement of words on the page is significantly less than half of the required effort.

The self-publishing world, or Indie publishing, as it's called, is like the Wild West. It's a free-for-all, but one that is at least vigorous and exciting. It's young, and things are happening in this wild place! You will need to stop worrying that being with all these other writer wannabes makes you look bad, and do what every writer needs to do—focus on your book and set yourself apart. Concentrate on finding a following of people who might want to hear what you have to say, who share your interests, who are attracted to your *platform*—more about this word in a later chapter. Anything goes now, and I like that. The old-line publishers have for too long masqueraded as the bastion of quality. Now the reader will make the choice again of what succeeds, and because there are so many inexpensive options for e-books—even free—it's possible that more people will be reading, since it's so much more affordable. When did the price of anything ever go down before?

No one will miss the old style bookstores more than I will, but the business model is changing, and they're no longer competitive. Over time, they'll become more specialized and smaller in scale, a niche, more than a mainstream business, which is sad.

Let's look at the new Indie business model. The landscape has quickly filled with what are now called subsidy publishers. A few of them have even been purchased by the old New York houses, who are probably wondering how best to use them.

For the writer, the system works like this: you sign up for a basic publishing package that can include a variety of other options as add-on costs. You will be uncertain which are meaningful, and you hope they will truthfully tell you which to add. In nearly every package, you will pay for your manuscript to be designed and formatted for Print on Demand, POD. This means that your finished book can be ordered in quantities of as few as one and shipped to readers anywhere for a moderate total cost. This is the new breakthrough in publishing. It means no inventory is required, therefore no more books to get moldy in your basement, and no more explaining that $12,000 dead loss in printing costs to your wife.

When you have arranged for a cover design, either from your own source or through your new subsidy publisher, (again for an extra fee), the book is uploaded to the printing house (Lightning Source, typically) and made available on Amazon and other retailers. Lightning Source (LSI) is the printer who will print a single copy of your book and ship it via UPS; hence the term, Print On Demand (POD). Once a month LSI pays your publisher what they received from Amazon (or Barnes & Noble, etc.), less the cost of printing and shipping, for those of your books that were sold. The publisher deducts its cut and sends the rest to you a month or two later.

Let's look at this more closely. Through the package you purchased, you have paid for all of the upfront costs of publishing your book, and given the subsidy publisher a profit on them as well, because he has marked up these costs, sometimes more than 100%. He will not be taking any of the risks on this publication. The publisher knows he has to make money on getting you into print, because the average self-published book only sells a small handful of copies and there's no guarantee he will make anything from his percentage of those sales. Now, on every subsequent book you sell forever, you will also divide those net proceeds with the publisher. This will typically be an amount approximately equal to what *you* get on each copy, although it varies. You should now be asking yourself why you're giving him this extra cut of your royalties. Haven't you already covered all his costs and given him a profit?

The short answer is that you are paying him for what he knows about the business that you don't.

Let's also consider Kindle and Nook sales. This requires two additional preparations of your manuscript, which you will pay for, either in the package or as an extra. If your book is a normal one of all or mostly text edition, you can opt for a 70% commission with Amazon on Kindle sales. Some publishers will take a cut of this and others will not. Personally, I see no justifiable reason that they should. You can expect that the e-book sales will furnish the majority of your income. I've found that on my non-fiction, book sales are nearly equal between print and Kindle, but with my fiction, Kindle and Nook outsell print by seven or eight to one. This is understandable because a print edition fiction book of mine costs three times what the e–book does. Therefore, do *not* neglect to have your book formatted for this segment of the business. It is already critically important and will only grow more dominant in the future.

These publishers understand that as a newcomer the business looks to you like an incomprehensible maze. Knowing the elements of this process is their strength. They believe that you will pay a substantial amount of money, ranging from moderate to obscene, for a package of services that includes the benefit of not having to learn how it's done yourself. If you opt for this, you will save yourself the trouble of learning the ropes, but if your book sells well, you will pay for it heavily in unnecessarily lost income.

I found in my own experience and talking with others that many times the quality of services offered by some subsidy publishers is inferior. For example, the interior design and layout of the books is often done by inexperienced staff people who have no esthetic sense about what they're doing. The cover designs can often be amateurish. Many decisions are made without consulting you. One person I know was told that his novel was formatted in a sans-serif font because that was the way they did all of them. Quite appropriately, he blew up. I can't think of any novel I've ever seen that was formatted with a sans-serif font **like this one**—**Calibri**. It has its uses, but it is not a book font.

Corners are cut that you would not allow had you known about them in advance. Consultation on design is minimal or nonexistent. Because you have many questions and are probably nervous about the outcome of this process, access to people within the subsidy-publishing house is usually limited. You will dial in by phone, and after choosing from several options, you'll be routed to someone's voice mail, but almost never to a real person. Some writers can wait weeks for a response. Other times you will also wait weeks for an email response. This practice is so widespread that it has to be intentional, a way of screening in itself. You can imagine that when new publishing clients are so typically anxious and inexperienced at the same time, the publisher can spend all his time answering what he considers to be dumb questions, and this would require more staff, who might have to be trained. This is almost understandable, if not reassuring as customer service, but the flip side is that if you have a real problem, or some grave error on your part or theirs that requires a quick response, you will find yourself shut out of the process, facing a wall of structured silence as things go to hell with your book inside.

Many people have told me that dealing with their subsidy publisher was the worst experience they'd ever had with a company in any field in their entire lives. I don't wish to overstate this argument, but this is a process designed entirely in favor of your publisher. They are relying on you to be too dumb or passive to realize how poorly they perform.

Another problem is bad advice. On print books you will face a crossroads that will probably not be explained to you, yet it is *critical* that you understand it in detail. Your publishing experience will succeed or fail based on your choices. This decision concerns *where you expect to sell your book*.

As I suggested above, like the old-line New York publishers, the retail bookstore business is undergoing a vast consolidation that will ultimately result in only a fraction of the current stores remaining, doing mostly a specialty business, for example, travel or children's books. If you decide you still wish to sell your book in a bricks and mortar setting, then you will need to set your discount at 50% or 55%, which is what they receive from New York. A lesser discount means they absolutely won't touch your book because they can't afford to. Moreover, since your book doesn't bear the imprint of one of these major publishers and is self-published, the stores will discriminate against you, thinking that it's worthless. You will also face great obstacles in getting it reviewed in the press. The prejudice against self-published books is still huge, and is not going away in a hurry. Your task is to ignore it.

Yet another obstacle is that you are not likely to have a return policy for unsold books, because as an individual, how can you handle the logistics of it? Without it, your book is either destroyed or donated if it doesn't sell in a reasonable period, assuming it even got into the bookstore at all.

So here's the key issue: you can set only one discount rate at Lightning Source, and it covers everyone who sells books at retail. Amazon is perfectly happy to sell your print book all day for a 20% discount, not 50% or 55%, although they'll gladly take that too if you have set that as the rate, thinking you're going to get into some bookstores. On a book that retails for $16.00, that means that (at a 20% discount) Amazon keeps $3.20 instead of $8.00 or $8.80 (at the bookstore discount rate of 50% or 55%). That is a huge difference. Before you read on, multiply that by the number of copies you expect to sell.

To understand this better, let's look at production costs. LSI is currently charging $.90 for the (paperback) cover and $.013 per page. If your book has 300 pages, that means LSI charges $.90 plus $3.90 per copy. That totals $4.80 to print and bind it. Now, if you have set the discount at 55% in the hope of selling it to bookstores, on your $16.00 retail book, Amazon will keep that and pay the printer LSI $7.20 net on each sale, out of which they deduct the printing cost, $4.80, so the net payment to your subsidy publisher is $2.40, which you will split about equally. You will walk away with around $1.20 per copy, which is not much different from what you would've gotten from a New York publisher, had they accepted you. Here is where my blatant prejudice becomes visible: I would like to make more per copy on the book that cost me a year of my life to write than what the UPS guy makes who spends forty seconds delivering it. Yes, I mean that! Not that UPS doesn't do a good job.

Had you decided that the bookstores were a waste of time and they were not likely to sell your book—and we've seen enough to think is good reason to take this view—and set the discount at 20% to Amazon, they would pay LSI $12.80 per book (out of the $16.00 sales price). The printing cost would be the same, $4.80. LSI then deducts that $4.80 and pays the publisher $8.00. Your take out of this is about $4.00, more than three times the $1.20 you would've gotten at the 55% discount.

I have heard that some subsidy publishers recommend that their clients set the discount at 55%. This is nothing short of naïve, bordering on psychotic, and it only caters to the writer's naïve hope that the bookstores will embrace his novel. Others have recommended 40%, for no reason that makes any sense, because that's twice the cut you need to give Amazon, and it will have the effect of getting you into no bookstore anywhere. The only conceivable justification for a discount of 40% is that it will encourage Amazon to discount the books to retail buyers. But if you have to rely on selling your product as a bargain item, blatantly discounted right out of the gate, it doesn't say much for its inherent quality. This is what I mean by bad advice.

Now let's take this perilous walk yet one step further. If you publish the book yourself and eliminate the subsidy publisher, you get the entire $8.00 per copy, using the 20% discount. Amazon and LSI get the rest, their fee for manufacturing and retailing the book for you. You get no personal service or advice, but how much did you get anyway and what was it worth if you got some? In going it alone, you will probably save no money in set up costs, but you are likely to get a better quality job because you'll hire skilled people and make your own esthetic choices. No third party will mark up these costs, and you'll definitely have more control over the total look and feel of your book. The presentation of it is critically important, because it is the appeal of the cover that will determine whether the reader looks inside, whether on the Amazon site or in a bookstore. Instead of someone telling you that every book they do is set up in sans-serif font, you can say, I want my book set up in twelve point Baskerville, for example, which is what you're reading now.

If you have only one book and plan to do no more, and it's not likely to sell well, the subsidy publisher route may still make sense for you. You can be a published author, sell a few books to friends and family, sell a few more on Amazon, and get on with your bucket list without having to learn a business you'll never pay much attention to again.

If, however, you're a serious author, whether you have only one book with some appeal, or you're planning a series that could sell, you're better off learning the nuts and bolts of self-publishing and doing it all yourself. You will need to understand that the promotion will all be up to you, just as it is for any new author published anywhere. I will talk more about that later. Once the pain of mastering the detail of putting out your book is over, you will own it outright, and control it forever. And you will never give anyone else a cut. LSI will charge you $12.00 a year to keep the print title active in their files. Amazon will charge you nothing to keep the Kindle edition alive. That is your only hard cost once it's published. The other expenses are percentages of each sale for the retailer on print copies (Amazon in most cases) and the manufacturing costs for each copy, as we have seen.

Here's what to do: learn the process of the Indie publishing business. I will explain the basics in a chapter below, and the Internet is full of sites that will tell you more of the detail.

That is the route I ultimately took. At first I found the process opaque, but the more time I spent on it the clearer it became. It will be much easier for you, because you now have this book in your hands.

The message is that it *can* be done, and done well without New York. Self-publishing demands the same things that other small businesses require: determination and hard work. Isn't that what writing the book also required? That's no coincidence, and if you got that part right, don't think for a moment that you lack the skills to master this next step.

22.

SELF-PUBLISHING

This chapter makes the assumption that you have read the previous chapter, titled Publishing Without New York, and decided to do it yourself, rather than use a subsidy publisher. This way you will owe no one a cut once you've paid the expenses of publication.

To self-publish your book in both print and e-book format, you will need the following items in this order:

1. A clean and edited finished manuscript.
2. A name for your publishing company and a logo.
3. A cover design, front and back.
4. Obtain an ISBN, the International Standard Book Number.
5. Have the interior formatted for Print on Demand.
6. Open an account at Lightning Source and upload the book.
7. Have the manuscript formatted for Kindle, Nook and any other e-book companies you plan to use.

Let's look at each of these in more detail.

A clean and edited finished manuscript. This means that your editor has been through it. You've made the desired corrections and your proofreader has worked it over, because the editor will usually not be the proofreader unless so specified. Many editors consider this to be an extra assignment. You are now happy with the result and have signed off on the contents of your book. Making changes once you've started the publication process can be costly and frustrating, so make sure you are really ready. Look at the detail of your book. Have you been consistent in the way you've handled its format? If you've left an intentional space between two paragraphs to indicate a shift of some kind, as in POV, has it been consistent throughout? Your editor may not realize it's her job to check things like this. Are the number of skipped lines between the chapter title and the first line of type consistent throughout?

Look at your front matter. This includes everything up to the first line of your text. The first page inside the cover should be what's called the half title. Only the title of the book appears on this page, no author name, nothing else. The title page is next, then come acknowledgements. Look at the acknowledgement pages of other books. Thank by name the people who helped you. Find a copyright format you like, and create your own that includes the date and disclaimers, and insert this below the acknowledgments. Below that place these letters: ISBN. Leave the rest of that line blank until you get the actual number. Put the URL for your website on this page at the bottom. Decide where you want your page numbers, title and author name in the body of the book. Confer over all this with your book's interior designer, who is also the person doing the POD format.

On the last page, about six or more lines after the final sentence, enter something like this: "Visit the author's website at **www.sanmiguelallendebooks.com**. This is not traditional, but it is your best moment to get your reader to look at your other offerings. If you don't have any, put it up anyway because down the road you may have some, and your book will be available for a long time.

A name for your publishing company and a logo. Be sure the name you choose is not in use. Look it up on the Internet. It should not be your personal name. When it comes to setting up your account at LSI, they want you to look like a real publisher, which you are, even if it's only for a single book of your own. The graphics person who designs your cover can supply your company logo. It should appear on the back of the cover and the bottom of the title page. If that person says he can't do logos, then you're dealing with a formula designer who lacks flexibility. Find someone else with an imagination.

A cover design, front and back. Don't be afraid to spend a little money on this, because no one will buy your book that isn't drawn in by the cover. It should please the eye and connect to the story inside. The color contrasts should make the spine easy to read, since that's all that will usually be visible on the shelf. The back should contain a one-paragraph biography of you with a headshot. If you have any brief blurbs, include them. The other paragraph will be a synopsis/plug for the book. Write these with care, and then revise them with even more care, with an eye to their impact on someone considering the purchase of this book. Look at the back of some other books you think are well designed, which is to say they please your eye and make you want to pick them up. Tell the graphics person the ISBN is coming so he should leave a space for it both as a number and a barcode. Once that is added and you're happy with the whole package, ask the designer to supply you with the finished cover as a pdf or jpeg image that includes front, back and spine, and a second image that is front only. The front image should come in two versions, one high resolution and the other medium. You will need it both ways. Putting it up on Nook, at Barnes & Noble, and sometimes on Facebook, requires the lower resolution image.

Obtain an ISBN, the International Standard Book Number. Sign on to Bowker and set up an account. http://www.bowker.com/en-US/. You can purchase any number of ISBNs, starting at $125 for one, $250 for ten, and so on. At a certain large quantity they cost only $1.00 each. Obviously you should get at least ten if you know you'll need more than one. Get what you think you're going to need. Once you've bought them, as you fill out the online form to enter a new title, you'll see the ISBN come up. Send it to your cover designer for the exterior. Get it right, because making a mistake in the ISBN here or later will snafu your efforts beyond your wildest dreams. Most cover designers can generate the bar code once they know the number. Once he has done this, he is nearly finished.

Have the interior formatted for Print on Demand. Unless you are skillful and experienced at using Adobe InDesign software, which is not the simplest of tools, don't attempt this yourself. It will literally determine every aspect of your book's interior appearance. Designers can be found on the

Internet who will do it for $3 to $10 a page. Ask to see excerpted samples of their work. Submit the manuscript as a Word.doc to the interior designer you select in the font and size you want. Discuss the font you'd like to use, and any other special details. Make sure both edges are justified. Enter the ISBN in the space you've left on your copyright page before you send it to the designer. Ask to see a sample of your first few pages once they set it up. Does the spacing between the lines, the leading, look right? There should be enough air in it to make for clear, easy reading. On the other hand, don't make the book any longer than you need because each page is costing you 1.3 cents on every copy you sell. It doesn't matter if they're blank.

When the interior is finished, it is formatted as a specific type of pdf that is required by Lightning Source in order to print it on demand. You will need to see this and proofread it before you give the final installment of the payment to the designer. Watch for proper spacing of words in a line, of justification on both margins, for consistency of format throughout. Watch to see that most widows and orphans have been eliminated: dangling words at the end of a paragraph or at the start of a new page. Sometimes changing a single word in the text will rectify this without damaging your meaning or style.

Cooperate with your designer. Hopefully, he has done this before many times. If he's a novice, don't use him, because you are too and you won't necessarily know when he's gone off the track. Two amateurs working together on your book will add up to a disaster. This is no time for improvisation.

<u>Open an account at Lightning Source and upload the book.</u> Go to <u>www.lightningsource.com/</u>. In the menu bar at the top go to New Client and follow the directions to open an account. Have a credit card ready. You will have already decided with your interior book designer to go for a 5.5 by 8.5 inch format in paperback, and this will govern the interior design. Always use cream paper, unless you've got color images. I don't recommend **POD** printing with color images because it adds a lot to the cost and the result will not usually look like a first class job. White paper is too bright and looks amateur.

<u>Have the manuscript formatted for Kindle and Nook.</u> Many people are able to do this, and you can find someone on the Internet and do it all by a keystroke. It requires knowledge of HTML, and it shouldn't cost much. I am presently paying $55 for a package of Kindle, Nook, and two other formats. Don't let someone charge you $175 or more. Once

you have these preps in hand, go to the Amazon and Barnes and Noble sites and open an account on each. Then upload your book following their instructions.

You will have already prepared a brief autobiography and a synopsis of the book to paste into the form to save time. Don't get too wordy because the reader will not spend a lot of time with them. Take care to make both appealing. This is pure advertising for yourself and your book. Show your accessible self in the bio, and write the brief synopsis as if it's the only chance you'll ever have to tell a potential reader about the book's contents. It may be exactly that. After all, you wrote this book partly for yourself, so think in terms of what's in it that would make you want to read it.

In dealing with all of these elements: Amazon, Nook, Bowker, and LSI, pay extreme attention to detail, and proofread what you've entered several times. Any errors can be rectified later, but if you discover a need for revision once you've submitted your book, changing the cover or text with LSI, for example, costs $40.00 apiece, and they will slow down the process. The basic set up at LSI costs $75.00, plus $40.00 for a proof copy, which I highly recommend. E-proofs are free. After that, you'll pay $12.00 a year to keep the book active in their files.

23

REVIEWS

Reviews are the posted public reaction of those who have read your book. If you are self-published, or published by one of the subsidy presses, you will find it nearly impossible to get your book reviewed by the conventional print reviewers. Here the prejudice still applies against anyone whose work does not emerge from a New York publishing house.

One option is to hire reviews on a fee basis. Often people who offer this service will also provide advertising on their review website. It's difficult to say what this might be worth. I tried it only once and was disappointed, even though the review I received was favorable. But my sample was hardly exhaustive. I would suggest trying it only on a very limited scale, and then watching the results closely. It should be possible to contact authors (through their own websites) whose work has been reviewed on these sites and ask them how they felt about the experience. Another program is *Good Reads*, one I haven't tried, although I know some people have had success with it. More will be developing all the time as the need for reviews for self-published books is always growing.

The mainstay of most self-published authors are the reviews on Amazon posted by people who have read the book either by purchasing it or obtaining it by other means. I make it a habit of asking people who I know have read my books to please put up a review on Amazon. Not many do, but you will get some response from this.

Go on Twitter and type in #review. You will find lists of people who review books. Your homework is to follow them, contact them, and see if they will review yours. Another hash tag to try is #blogger. Some people, like Amanda Hocking, have been hugely successful getting lots of reviews, but I think it's gotten more difficult now. Bloggers and reviewers are getting backed up with the enormous volume of self-published books. Some successful authors have bought positive reviews by the hundred, but Amazon is cracking down on that and is far more vigilant about reviews that appear to be mass-produced. You will often now see the phrase at the top of a review, *Amazon Verified Purchase*. This means that the reviewer paid for his copy of the book, whether in Kindle or print. Amazon keeps good records.

What happens if somebody dumps on your book? Most writers will advise patience and forbearance. You will not please every reader, and for some commentators, the fact that a reviewer hated your book is a sign that you have found a focused audience, one that excludes that reader. Other writers just ignore all the reviews as not being germane to their process. I rarely read them except for an occasional quick scan to see whether the trend favors high ratings. For me, this is the bottom line.

Amazon provides a function where you can request a review be eliminated, but it rarely works. If you do get a severely negative review, particularly one that uses your book as a prime example of the deteriorating condition of western civilization, check out that person's other reviews by clicking the link at the bottom of the review. You will most likely find that he dumps on everything that moves. He also hates his air conditioner and his coffee pot. It comes from his mental condition, and one way of feeling better about himself is to be proven superior to the rest of the world, which has consistently let him down at every turn. That's most easily done by judging it worthless. There are also many people out there who feel themselves principled, but are really only judgmental.

Reviews are your way of knowing approximately what your readership thinks of your work. This information is useful, but don't let it sway what you do. The direction of your course as a writer is best determined by you alone. Paying too much attention to what everybody else thinks is a way of producing work they all expect, which is not, in my view, a good direction to take. Aim to surprise your readers, not by scooting off on a tangent, but by intensifying and elevating to a new level those aspects of your work that attracted them in the first place. Making them stretch as you do will keep them loyal.

PART THREE

MARKETING YOUR BOOK

24.

E-BOOK PRICING

Although the title may not sound like it, this chapter is really part of marketing, because that's what e-book pricing is all about. Print copy pricing will be determined by your New York publisher, if you have one, or by your printing and distribution costs if you are self-publishing. That issue, with its discounts, has been covered in another chapter.

Take some time exploring the Amazon site in detail. Begin the e–book process by using your publishing name to open an account at Amazon, and then go to your dashboard to put up your book.

Because the cost structure is entirely different with e–books, pricing is geared to address the niche you occupy in your market. Amazon, the chief player for e–books, offers two levels of commissions. If you have a book that is filled with illustrations, photos, graphs or charts, the size of the Kindle e–book file that Amazon transmits to the customer will be large. If your book is normal, and almost all or entirely text, that expense is not significant. If you opt to pay this cost yourself on each sale, you can select 70% of the retail price as commission on each sale. The transmission cost will be deducted from this. If you wish Amazon to pay that cost, they will require you to select a 35% commission.

But how do you know which one to choose? When you enter your book's information on the Kindle set-up site, you can test the outcome both ways. By the time you reach that point, you will have already uploaded your prepared Kindle book file (Mobi), so Amazon knows how big it is. Enter 70% for the commission and the grid will show your net return, after transmission costs are deducted. Then change the commission to 35%, which will be that percentage of retail with the transmission cost borne by Amazon, in other words, with no deductions. You are not locked into anything at this point, and in both cases the form will display your projected net return. Which is your greater profit per e–book? Usually, the 70% commission, minus the transmission costs, will work best for you unless your file is exceptionally large. Select the larger commission outcome for yourself and move to the next point on the form.

For my books, which are all text with no graphs or photos, the transmission cost ranges from five to six cents per Kindle copy. Across my sixteen published books, all of which are on Kindle, the manuscript size varies from 55,000 words on the smallest, to 105,000 words on the largest. For reasons I'll explain below, I price all my e-books at $5.99, so my profit is 70% of $5.99, or $4.19, minus $.05 on most books, or minus $.06 on the larger ones. Obviously, transmission costs would have to be quite large to make the 35% commission rate a better choice. Note that Amazon does not offer the 70% option on Kindle books priced under $2.99. Setting a price below that level will always yield a 35% commission to you.

For a long time the extremely successful e-book author, John Locke, whom I speak about again in the next chapter on the subject of his blog, priced all his e-books at $.99, and sold millions of copies. He made $.35 per Kindle book. Then he changed his pricing to $2.99, where he collected 70%, or $2.10, less no more than $.05 for transmission costs. He now makes about six times as much per copy. If the price increase caused a 50% drop in sales, he is still making three times as much as before the price change. But I doubt that such a drop occurred. His market was well established when he made the change, and how many of his readers were really going to object to paying $2.99 per book for a series they love? I suspect that the largest loss for Locke was among incoming readers who had not read his books before. Some of these folks are committed to the $.99 price bracket and will not go above it.

We can see from this that making money on Kindle is dependent upon maximizing dollar returns more than the number of books sold. You need to tune your price to your market. As with Locke, pricing strategy is critical, and I believe it was part of his strategy to wait until a substantial number of readers were deeply involved in his series of thrillers before he made the change.

Since I have a series of ten mysteries available, and the number is constantly growing, I decided to use the first one, *Twenty Centavos*, as a low-price leader to entice people into the series. For a while I priced it at $.99. I then tracked sales of the second book, at $5.99, relative to the first. What kind of follow through was I getting? The answer was that 24% bought the second book, *The Fifth Codex*, at six times the cost. How to interpret that? I made the assumption that almost all of these people who bought the second had bought the first book too. I was making $.35 on each Kindle sale of *Twenty Centavos* at $.99. If it went to $5.99, like the rest of the

series, and I made $4.14 after costs on each copy, that
would be 11.33 times the profit on each book. But
what would happen to the sales volume, not only on
the first, but the follow through as well? In ways most
writers don't want to think about, selling e–books
is a numbers game, and your financial survival as a
writer depends on your skill at playing it.

What happened when I changed the price
to the same level as the others was that the sales
of *Twenty Centavos* dropped by 60%, but the follow
through sales of the second book, *The Fifth Codex*,
dropped only by 10% in absolute numbers. What did
this mean?

Surely, as I speculated with John Locke's sales,
there is a group of e–book buyers out there that will
pay no more than $.99, and the change in price had
left most of those behind. Usually, even if they like
the first one, they won't buy the next one in the series
for $5.99. It's price loyalty, not brand loyalty. But the
point of this game is to get the buyer into the series
and buy all ten books, so the reader who buys the
second one is likely to go on, and will spend far more
than the cost of the first two books.

My market research on this issue suggests
that there may be a perception among some e–book
buyers, ones who can spend more, that a $.99 book

isn't worth much, on the theory that you get what you pay for. That buyer, the one willing to spend $5.99, was the one I wanted to keep, since I had ten books for sale in that series. On the other hand, many well-known authors are pricing their Kindle and Nook books at $12.99, a price that is too steep for lesser or unrecognized authors. A friend of mine with no track record in fiction published a fine first novel but set the Kindle edition price at $9.99. This is a bit high for a book by an unknown author. If your name is not a household word, try the $5.99 level, which is no more than a low-level hurdle, but be ready to experiment. These prices will speak to readers with different mindsets. You can pull up your Amazon bookshelf page and make price changes at any time. In my experience, your book is usually off the market for only a couple of hours when you do this. My sense is that $5.99 provokes little price resistance, even as it suggests there is some value to the book. Yahoo has a self-publishing group that you can join and learn a great deal by tracking the discussion of this and related issues. Again, if you are published in New York, you will not have much choice in pricing and you'll be giving a percentage of the e–book revenue to your publisher. Should that be the case, take a hard look at how much you're giving away. E–books represent no investment for the New York publisher beyond formatting—perhaps $50 per book at most, and probably less. Many will also make it hard for you to know your sales, which are visible only to the publisher. If you self-publish, you can watch them tick by tick.

And then there are the free books. What is that about? If you join Amazon's KDP Select system, which lasts 90-days in renewable segments, you will agree to loan out your book at no charge to Select members, and in return receive a share of a big monthly payout based on the number of times your book was loaned. I do it on Twenty Centavos because it seems like a decent deal and a way to increase circulation and name recognition. Most authors who use this program do it because it also allows them to give away their e–book for up to five days out of the ninety in each period. If you do this, Amazon requires that you withdraw your book from avail-ability on any other e–book site. It's easy to calculate what this costs in lost sales.

Why would you give your book away? The logic is multi-layered. If you have a series, like I do, giving the first one away gets the reader painlessly in the door. Of course, there is still that taint of cheap-ness to factor in, and there are many readers out there who subsist only on giveaway books, and are therefore no use to you as potential buyers of the rest of your series. But this still costs you nothing. If you have only one book, it may still make sense to give it away because Amazon has some in-house promotional benefits that you will receive if you can give enough e-copies away. The last time I tried it the magic number was about 750 giveaway books during the period you offer it, one to five days. If you hit this level they will send out emails to promote your book once the price returns to normal. If you don't hit it, the effort was largely useless, but like many things you do for promotion, you can't easily tell ahead of time how it will work. A variety of websites exist that will advertise your freebie. Plug in *giveaway books* and see what you come up with. Find some freebie sites online and give them advance notice, which they need to feature your giveaway. If you do give books away, be sure to download one for yourself, not that you need it, but that way you can track whatever promotion Amazon does for you later as follow through. You don't have to use your five free days all at once, but it probably works best if you do, so you have a greater chance of hitting the magic volume number to trigger their promotion. Make sure the five days includes a weekend. As a way of supporting your promotion, Amazon charges no transmission costs on free e–books. These programs are subject to periodic change, so check the rules before you get into this. The anticipation is that Amazon will tweak this program or launch others in the future, so find out the current details before you start.

25.

BUILDING A PLATFORM

If you decide to approach an agent with your completed and edited manuscript, assuming you reach the point of having a conversation, one of the first questions she will ask is, "What is your platform?" Knowing what this means and having one in place will place you a major step ahead of the game. Your platform is a fundamental tool you will need to promote your work, no matter which route to publication you choose. If you're trying to sell your book in New York, no one there will help you assemble it, and not having one in place will make that sale less likely.

Think of your platform as the way of generating a presentation to your target reader. Start by taking a look again at those elements that make your book what is. Draw up a list of them. With my own first mystery, *Twenty Centavos*, such a list would look like this:

Mystery, detective (#1 in a series)
Art, artist
Mayan antiquities
México, travel
México, expat living

The first question in building a platform becomes this: how do you reach people with all or some of this set of interests, in other words, your target reader? You already know what she looks like because you've given her some serious thought before you started the book. Now that you're finished, she's still around and ready to make herself useful in this next phase.

The México themes offer the most important pair on this list. I already follow several different websites that feature subjects related to México. Why not start my own, in effect, by blogging about México and expat life, as well as writing? After six years of living here, it's a subject I know first hand, and one I've developed some strong feelings about, largely because the American press has so distorted the subject. A reader interested in what it's really like to live as an American south of the border might also enjoy reading mysteries. When these two interests overlap, bingo! I am effectively approaching this reader from two directions at the same time.

John Locke, the writer who has been enormously successful in selling e-book thrillers, lists blogging as his number one promotional idea. Look up his website and examine what he does in his blogs that gives him this kind of momentum. Here's the link: www.donovancreed.com.

One way he works is to include the names of famous people in his posts so that if someone searches that name online, Locke's blog has a good chance of coming up in the result. One example he used early on, before the Penn State scandal broke, was Joe Paterno.

There are many free blog hosts on the Internet, and setting up a page of your own is easy. Give it a title that connects to your platform so when people put in search words they may be brought to your site. My blog is titled *An American Voice in México*. I just did a Google search on this phrase and my blog was the third item on the first page that came up. The other two were recent news items about the death of the singer, Jenny Rivera.

The strategy is an interesting one, because it is not like conventional advertising. The approach is to provide real and usable content for your reader that is both an example of your interests and a sample of your writing style. It is your product in itself, in miniature, and it is not a billboard urging the reader to rush out and buy your book. But at the end of the blog, you will include your website URL, your Twitter handle, and your Facebook address. You don't have any of these? Your book cannot be a bestseller unless people know about it, and word of mouth is not sufficient. You will find plenty of material online about setting up all of these: your Twitter page, your blog site, and your Facebook account.

What I found shortly after I started blogging was that some of the México websites began picking up my postings and republishing them without any effort on my part. This told me two things: my content was of broad enough interest to appeal to their readership, and this was an excellent way of multiplying my website traffic. The next step was obvious; I began to search out other México websites, and submitted material to them. This was how I found Mexconnect, the largest online magazine on the subject of México. It has between 300,000 and 500,000 visitors a month, with more than a million individual article hits. I sent off two articles and they bought both of them. I soon followed with others. In this way I became a regular feature writer for the magazine. As of this writing, they have also reviewed two of my books in the feature position on page one. More reviews are coming.

The material I supply them is always focused and specific. The first articles included *Driving in México: No Country for New Cars* (a humorous piece), one on junkyards as the place to find the real México, another on the meaning of being an expat, including safety issues, and a fourth on expat life in a nearby recovering ghost town called Pozos, once a mining bonanza site. Notice that I don't do typical travelogues. The style is narrative rather than declarative, and never top heavy with data. The geography is off the beaten path. Information is worked naturally into the flow of the story when it's relevant. I am present in a limited way in all of them. Rather than generalize, I use the kind of detail that I wrote about in fiction in an earlier chapter. None of them contain a direct pitch for any of my books. The point is to establish a presence and to have my name associated with the subject of being an American writer living south of the border.

An important feature is that these pieces are as polished as any of my book-length work. Remember, they serve as samples of what I do. If the readers enjoy them, if they look for a new piece by me in each issue, then they are likely to check out my website and look at my books as well. It is subtle and without pressure. The platform is the stage you will stand on to present yourself, and it is partly no more than your identity as expressed by your interests and writing style.

The Internet is full of websites catering to specific interests. They can provide you with access to a highly focused audience in any area. Not all of them solicit articles from the public, but many of them do. If your main character is a cat-lover, for example, you can seek out sites that cater to people with a similar interest and approach them about using some articles from you. Perhaps you own an exotic breed. Study other examples of what the website is publishing and figure out how yours can be similar enough to be included, yet distinctively yours. At the bottom of your submission place a link that says, "Jane Doe's new book, (title & website link) reveals facts about cat ownership you've never heard before."

If woodworking is an important element in your story, which has as its main character a great custom furniture designer-builder, there are plenty of sites dealing with that. Submit something useful to some of them, but don't duplicate it to different sites. Suppose you know that lemon juice takes the purplish stains off your hands after you've worked with black walnut. Talk about that, and about how some exotic woods, like cocobolo, one of the rosewood family, can cause allergic reactions when its sawdust comes in contact with your skin. Try to offer information most people don't know. The whole point is that whatever your book may feature is a potential area for you to link up with other people in a blog or an article for someone else's website. Your blogs should be informal and enjoyable. Allow your enthusiasm to show. Even though you're an author, you are also human and vulnerable, so be accessible. If your blogs have a stiff tone, you can shoot yourself in the foot by putting readers off. It's not a bad idea to have a link so the blog reader can contact you. A personal response will often make that person a fan.

Many, but not all of these sites, offer reviews of books connected to the site's theme. When you see that, make sure the reviewer gets a copy of your book. If it's not available in print, find out whether the reviewer will take a Kindle copy and gift him one if he will.

These are only a few possible features of your platform, but think of the process as taking up prominent positions in the middle of your fields of interest. Make yourself noticeable.

Yahoo offers many user groups. You can find

a list of them online. Many do not permit direct advertising, but it still makes sense to join several related to subjects or locations connected to your book. Participate frequently in their discussions online, again, adding useful content. Formulate your automatic signature block to look something like this:

John Scherber
Author of *San Miguel de Allende: A Place in the Heart*
WEBSITE: www.sanmiguelallendebooks.com
BLOG: http://www.blogster.com/johnscherber
TWITTER: @MEXTEXT

Then, every time you send a comment, the signature block appears beneath your name and includes your message. You should have it on all your regular email as well.

Similarly, local organizations may exist in your town that relate to your subject. They often present speaking opportunities. I once addressed Rotary with a reading and commentary from my book on the expat experience. I sold thirteen autographed copies and shook a lot of hands afterward. People I meet still tell me that they heard that talk, even though it's been more than three years ago now. Writer's groups and libraries may also offer public readings. Meeting the author can be important for people who are avid readers. If reading the book is a personal encounter with the author's ideas, you can imagine that meeting the author in person is even more so.

Feel free to talk about your experiences in writing, learning your craft, books you're working on now, and books you'd like to write. Many readers would like to get inside your head. Let them ask questions. Ask some in return and solicit their suggestions. As your readers, it's always useful when you can learn more about them and what they appreciate about your books.

If you're not at ease speaking at length, turn the occasion into a Q and A session after some preliminary remarks, and people will rise to the opportunity to speak to you one on one. Have a friend in the audience ready to ask a question if no hands go up right away. It might require a little priming of the pump. Some people would like to ask their question, but aren't comfortable going first in case it doesn't seem as intelligent as others that follow.

You will often get comments on your blog site, if it has this function and your topics are stimulating. Be sure to choose a site host that allows this. Respond to these, addressing people by name. Make sure you have a contact button on your website so people can send you an email. When they do, reply in a welcoming fashion, even if their comments are sometimes surprising. Your underlying message should be that you welcome their input and you value the fact that they took time to send you a message. You'll pick up a few strange comments, but that's part of the game.

Many writers shrink from the prospect of putting themselves forward constantly. It may seem unbecoming or pushy. Maybe they weren't raised that way, or are simply shy. After all, writing is an excellent job for loners, even if it rarely pays well. The fact remains that you are the best person to get your message out there. You can go broke hiring someone else to do it, and still get little effect. If you send a note to a writer you enjoy, how wonderful is it to get a note back from his publicist? You know the writer never saw what you wrote. Your readers will want to meet you and shake your hand.

No one was more reluctant to get into promotion than I was. I resented the time it took from my writing. I wasn't sure how well I'd be accepted. Now I've come to enjoy it, and I see it as an integral part of writing as a job and a business. Without it, no one would know about my work. As you do it more, it'll get easier too, and it will feel more relaxed and natural. After all, aren't you the one who needs to be heard and read? Make that part of your persona.

I was once at a large party and a woman I didn't know came up to me and asked if I was John Scherber. When I admitted that I was, she introduced herself with, "I'm your biggest fan!" I knew than that my promotional efforts were paying off.

The social media, mainly Twitter and Facebook, are additional ways to build your platform. There are a number of others, and the list grows all the time. Do some research online. Your blog site should offer at the end of each of your blogs a chance for you to put that posting up on Twitter and Facebook. Mine also displays more than 180 other links for me to use in sharing my views.

I use Facebook in a variety of ways. I post information about what I've been up to recently. For example, I made a trip to the Yucatán to research backgrounds for my eleventh mystery. I posted photos and simple comments about the images, subtly mentioning from time to time why I was there. Covers of coming books go up as a teaser, and I always mention the release date. I try to stay away from politics and I never post prepared banners with slogans or tidbits of someone else's wisdom. I want all content to come from me because it's part of my platform.

One exception is that I do relay links to

published articles from time to time that take a sane outlook on the idea of living in México. Many people are spooked by the crusading rants of the US press, and it's good to offer some more realistic alternative views. Initially I struck back with some angry, combative pieces, but after a while I responded simply by showing in my México lifestyle posts the kind of normal existence I lead in this country.

I also offer links on Facebook to my new blog posts when they come out, and to my articles on Mexconnect. Occasionally I post covers of existing books with a small, riveting excerpt. I usually have my website URL included at the bottom of my own posts. Comment on your Facebook friends' posts as a way keeping your name current. It pays to experiment. Many publications and articles exist with more suggestions than I can provide here, and the terrain changes often. Take a look at your book from a variety of angles and be creative. Survey what other people are doing that effectively draws your eye. At present I don't have an author page, so all this is done on my personal page. Use www.facebook.com/john.scherber to friend me.

On Twitter the task is to use the 140 character maximum length creatively and to your advantage. I post a link to my current blog every day at varying times, and I always retweet people who have retweeted me.

Once you've signed up and chosen a name, get started by looking at the followers of people who share your interests. Follow those who look like a potential match. There is a space at the top of your page where you can enter hash tags to search for them. For example, #mexico. A list of tweets will appear that include that word. Follow those who look interesting, which is to say that they might find you interesting too. For me, this one alone was a great opportunity. Go online and search *hash tag lists*. You will be given lists to choose from to get hash tags that connect to your platform. Use them in the search engines on Twitter. I also follow other writers through #amwriting, for example. Most people will follow you back, especially once you get a few hundred other followers. Within current rules you will come under some constraints once you are following 2,000 people. After that you will be limited to following only 10% more than are following you.

When I hit this limit it slowed me down considerably. The solution is that you can buy followers. Search *buy Twitter followers*. Is this kosher? I don't care. It's not murder and we talked about shades of gray earlier. I bought 1,000 followers for $14.00. I'm not sure who they are, and I don't believe they care much about me, but I received around 1,400 within three days and didn't loose many by having them unfollow me. Most important, what I got from the purchase was the ability to continue following people with my range of interests, because the 1,400 I received gave me the ability to follow 1,540 more (110%) who were focused on what I do. Since most followed me back, I'm still way ahead of the game and have not hit any limits since. Nor have I bought any more followers.

Fourteen dollars is not a budget-buster. At this point I've spent right around $100 on promotional costs. I've been working it hard for twenty months. The conclusion is clear: it's all about time and effort and accumulating insight as you go. The money required will not be nearly as excessive as the time. A few promotional experts that I talked to before I started wanted to try it for me, but didn't have any direct experience with books. One knew everything about yoghurt. Another who had done books before, wanted six thousand dollars to do press releases and send review copies—the old style of book marketing. It's a highly specific field, changing daily, and I turned them all down. I didn't want them to teach themselves the business on my dime.

The promotional track is clearly different

depending on whether you are self-published or conventionally published, but in both cases be prepared to do it all yourself.

To my Twitter followers I also send a daily link to my current blog, but at different times of the day. They scroll past rapidly and you'll catch a different crowd at six in the morning from the one you reach at lunch or dinner. On my blog site traffic screen I can track how many hits I get when I post a tweet link. Usually I'll get twenty to thirty hits in the next ten minutes. On heavier traffic days, like weekends, I'll bring up older posts and tweet the links again. This works well, especially since I'm adding new followers all the time, and for them it's new material. My website link is provided at the bottom of every blog post.

Amazon, one of the most marketing-savvy firms on earth, also provides links on the page of your book for Twitter, Facebook, and others. Click on these connections and it opens your account at Twitter, for example, with a link to the book and some catchy phrase you can add in the forty to sixty characters remaining. They are making it so easy for you! From watching the numbers I know that Sunday evening is the biggest sale time for my Kindle books. I'm not sure why, but I don't have to know to act on that. I often use the Amazon links to bring the covers forward, book by book starting on Sunday afternoon. Twitter will not allow you to tweet the same thing more than once a day. You'll need to add some variety anyway so your followers don't get bored. Don't forget to mix in useful information that does not directly promote you.

When you use this Amazon link to bring your book page up on your Facebook page, it delivers the cover image and a blurb. The image is the link for the reader to click on. Add your own comments above. Don't miss out on this free and easy opportunity. And don't be misled by people who portray Amazon as a villain. It uses a new and aggressive way of doing business that is causing havoc in New York. By opening the door to a lot of writers who would not otherwise find a market, its efforts on behalf of self-published authors have been a lifeline to the reading market. I always look forward to my bank deposit from them in the last week of every month.

As I noted above with Facebook, volumes of resources exist on how to use Twitter. Many are worth looking at and spending a few dollars on, although most the information can be had for nothing by spending sometime with your Internet search engine. They can save you time and focus your efforts where the results will be best. Some writers will have a Facebook page for each of their books. That may be worth looking into.

Here in my town of San Miguel de Allende, we have a civil list, a Yahoo group. It's a bulletin board for issues related to our lives here, and currently it reaches eight thousand subscribers, many of whom live in the United States. A little direct marketing is permitted, although not much. I take an active role in posting on this list, putting up my books once a month. I especially like to answer questions from newcomers or others that are contemplating a move to México. Naturally, my signature block lists my expat book and my website. If your book has a geographic connection to a place that has a Yahoo group list, it will be worth joining. It is a collection of people with a focused interest in what you are doing. Look it up on Yahoo groups.

I dealt with blogs briefly above, but I want to end by saying a few more words about them. Because I enjoy doing pieces about the writing process, about half my blog posts focus on aspects of the writing life. The other half is about the expat lifestyle in México. I try to put up a new post about twice a month. That doesn't swamp the reader, and it's not too demanding of my time. On average they run about 1200 words and it takes me an hour and a half to write and revise one. Sometimes they mention my books, other times they don't, but the website and other links are always at the bottom of the post. Here's an example of a mention within that post I referred to above, titled, *Driving in México—No Country for New Cars*. This is the final paragraph of the piece:

A final word about parking. Someone once asked me how my detective, Paul Zacher, always finds a parking place in San Miguel. "That," I replied, "is why it's called fiction."

This was a humorous piece about the fear people often have of driving in México. The mention of the mysteries at the end is gentle, and it fits completely into the context of the rest of the article. If you want to put in a plug for your work, keep it at this level, inoffensive and subtle. People won't mind. Even as a plug, this sentence still provides an accurate comment about parking, and the purpose of these blogs is always to convey useful information that illustrates your writing style and personality. Blogs are informal; they should allow the reader to glimpse the person you are in a way that may be more direct than in a book, and always engaging. Remember how we talked about relatability in your characters? Your writing persona needs to possess this feature as well. Your voice on the page should convey this.

My writing posts address the problems, concerns, and insights I've had in working my way through eighteen books. Because I've "followed" and "friended" a lot of writers on Twitter and Facebook, their common concerns are a great fit for my platform. Look at #self-publishing on Twitter.

How well do any of these things work? The answer is that I'm not sure. The only measure I have is that my sales continue to grow each month, but which effort is more effective than another in making this happen, I can't say. I wish I could, because I'm sure they don't all work equally. My strategy has been to imagine my target readers, and then to find and reach out to them.

I've heard that it takes three years to figure out effective marketing and get some results. As of this writing I've been at it for twenty months and I already know it's working. Like everything else in this business it's about hard work and persistence. Does it take seeing your name ten times connected with interesting content before people start to recognize it on Twitter or a blog post or Facebook? I can believe that it does. Give them a memorable shortcut.

As I mentioned above, I have characterized myself on my blog site as *An American Voice in México*. It's a label I encourage people to use in thinking about who I am and what I do. It says that I'm an expat living in México and that I speak out about the experience, whether through my books, blogs or magazine articles.

As a writer, what is *your* label? Your voice is as distinctive as mine or anyone else's, and readers will find it reflected in the content and style of your book(s). You can find a label for it that distills into a few words the essence of the way you wish to identify yourself. The key feature is that it be aimed at your target reader.

When your prospective agent asks you what your platform is, your response to the above elements will provide the answer. Even if you are skipping the agent/New York route, your platform needs will be the same. Just as in the chapter on tone and voice, or the chapter on developing character, the requirement is that you know who you are and can express that knowledge in an appealing way to potential readers. Normally labeling each other is a way of dismissing someone you don't agree with. In this case, make up the label yourself and hang it around your neck. It will give people a shorthand to recognize you and what you're up to. Put it at the top of your blogs and at the bottom of your signature block on email.

A final word on timing. Do not wait for your book to be finished and published before you build your platform. It should already be in place and growing in traffic when the book hits the marketplace. It's hard to promote it if there's no one waiting for it and no one already reading your posts. In addition to your normal blog posts, why not publish a few brief excerpts as teasers on your blog, maybe one a month over the last few months before publication? Use the same concepts as in ending a chapter, so that each excerpt can have the feel of leading to something that can only be found in the book itself.

26.

YOUR WEBSITE

I made brief mention above of your website, another hurdle, but a necessary one in the author's footrace. This is your showcase. Here you will stand alone with your background, your accomplishments, and your offerings. It's where you send people when they want to take a closer look at what you have to offer, like when they have finished reading your blog and find it insightful and amusing—not a bad combination, by the way. Now they are asking themselves, what else has this person done?

That is the desired effect. As a prime example of what comes next I offer a direct link to my own website: www.sanmiguelallendebooks.com.

Start here at the home page, with a benign photo of the author, and good, colorful graphics overall. Make sure your author shot looks sane and approachable. In my case, it's an inviting entry point that presents a whole range of books with varying content. Important here are the four links at the bottom of the page, and these links should be a key menu item on your website. These will take you to Twitter, Facebook, my blog site and Barnes & Noble's Nook. The Buy Online page has a button on each title that takes you to the Amazon page.

Visit the menu bar at the top. You are now at HOME, so go next to TITLES. You will see seventeen books displayed there, including this one, organized into nonfiction, mysteries, vampire, and thrillers. If this was your site, here is where the care you took with your cover design will pay off. Even if you have only a single book, you will need this page to feature it. This is one of the places that will benefit from one of those high-resolution front covers I mentioned earlier. Notice again the same four links at the bottom. In small type above the links are listed all the titles. When you click on any title, you move to an individual book page with a synopsis—the same effect you get when you click on the cover above.

Move to the next offering at the menu bar. Here is ABOUT JOHN SCHERBER. It's a brief biography that suggests what the author thinks he is trying to do and where he came from. Call it human interest and move on, picturing your face over his, but notice the same four links at the bottom as you do. PRESS AND BOOKINGS will offer any blurbs that people have been induced to offer for any of these books. Note this understandable fact: many authors much bigger than you will plant blurbs on the back of your (self-published) book if you ask them, because every copy you manage to sell is one more recommendation for their book. It's a way for them to hook into your audience, which presumably overlaps with theirs.

Here's an example, supplied by Tony Cohan, for my book on the expat experience, *San Miguel de Allende: A Place in the Heart*. He is well known for his book, *On Mexican Time*, as well as several others. "An attentive and richly stimulating series of interviews with North Americans who have made lives for themselves in another country, another town."

Don't be afraid to approach other authors with this request. The worst case is they'll ignore you.

The next item on the menu bar is CONTACT. Here you can email me to make comments on what you've read, or to find out when the next mystery is coming out. Anything is welcome. Once again, you will find the four key links at the bottom and the list of clickable titles. Next you can proceed to LINKS. Here you will find a connection to anyone I cared to promote and who wished to promote me on their site.

Next is the biggest link of all, **BUY ON LINE.** Here are all the covers. Click on any one and you are transported to the book detail, with the cash register and the little shopping cart at Amazon. If you click on **PUBLISHING SERVICES** you are taken to a page that lists services my wife and I provide for fee-based self-publishing aids, with no percentage of your book afterward.

Notice that navigation among all these pages is easy and intuitive. The reader can be at the individual Amazon page for any of these books in half a heartbeat.

Your website will look much different from mine because you will have given considerable thought on how to shape it to the specific virtues of your book or books. Research the websites of authors who have books in the same category as yours. You can get this from Amazon. See what attracts you and what doesn't. You and your web designer can decide how to use similar devices to the ones that work, without directly copying the websites you like.

When finished it should have the same strong points: visual attractiveness and ease of use. Looking at mine, try to think what I might have missed that you'd like to have on yours. Are you looking for something you don't see? This is your chance to do anything you want. Show mine to your website designer and ask him how he can improve on it. Ask him for his own ideas, given what you'd like to accomplish. Again, using a web designer with experience is important. You don't want someone practicing on what is your principal public image, and if you've never had a website before, you won't automatically know what you need.

PART FOUR

PERFECTING YOUR CRAFT

27.

WRITING CREDENTIALS

When I still lived in St. Paul, I took painting lessons from a woman I met with once a week. I would bring in a canvas that I'd been working on to show her and she'd critique it, gently commenting on my drawing, composition and color design. A private lesson appealed to me because I was too shy to be part of a class and risk looking foolish to people twenty years younger than I was, and who were also mostly better painters. She had a bachelor's degree in fine art and showed her work in a local gallery. She didn't fully make a living by her painting, but she sold pictures regularly, and she did bring in some decent money. This impressed me until I learned that she was also getting her MFA, a master's degree in art.

"Why would you need to do that," I asked, "when you can already paint, and people buy your work all the time? What other reason is there to do this? Does it get you a better price?" I considered her current position to be the desired reality in the art world, and even years later, I don't think that idea was wrong.

She couldn't explain why beyond the fact that she felt she needed a more advanced degree. She didn't say she needed learn how to paint *better*, which I assumed would develop mainly by painting more. Wasn't practice a big part of that picture?

You can call having the MFA a higher level of validation, if validation is a type of mantle that is conferred on you by accredited people, but to me the art sales were validation enough, in fact, they meant far more than any degree. She had found an audience, and she had told me that some people owned more than one of her works, so she was being *collected*.

This experience got me thinking about the difference between validation and performance.

In college I was an English major with a "concentration" in creative writing. It was true only in the sense that I had concentrated on it a great deal. Upon graduating, my degree gave me some validation, but I didn't learn enough in those five years to make me able to write two good novels later instead of the two bad ones I did write. In fact, even then I realized I had learned little beyond what I had already known going in. Was I really that much smarter than the courses I took and the professors that I listened to? No, as I subsequently learned, it was more that I wasn't getting what I thought I was paying for—a pathway to becoming a skilled and successful writer.

I was mainly an excellent wordsmith. I could craft a great line or paragraph, generate snappy dialog, and include enough offbeat turns to keep the reader engaged most of the time. What I did not know, and was unaware that I didn't know, was how to structure and build a good book. By being a life-long reader, I had learned many things about writing, but I still didn't know some of the basic mechanics of what I was trying to do.

So, what were my professors teaching me?

I will name my professor at the University of Minnesota, "Dr. Jones," because he may still be alive and I don't want to call him to account in his twilight years. He was known as a critic more than as a writer. It was a period when deconstructionism was in vogue, and he considered himself part of that movement. I didn't understand it, and I won't try to explain it now because it was a fad whose time has come and gone. You can find many articles about it on the Internet, and I recommend them for late night reading when you can't get to sleep any other way. What I realized as I listened to Dr. Jones talk about it was that nothing in it would ever apply to the physical and mental process of writing a book, except one on the subject of literary criticism. It was as abstract as ozone. I knew it was out there, but I could never find any way to connect with it. Yet seminar after seminar was absorbed into this vacuum. Perhaps my writing has suffered from the lack of attention I gave this subject, but I can truthfully say that not a single time in all the words I've put on paper since then have I ever thought of it again, until I started writing this chapter. Yet, having passed these courses with As and Bs, I was a *validated* writer. From my current perspective, I knew almost nothing. This is one reason I tend to be skeptical today of credentials.

A second component in this process went on at the same time and dovetailed perfectly with deconstructionism to obstruct useful learning. It was the implicit failure, or worse, the *refusal*, to treat writing as a craft. A craft, after all, is labor done within the framework of a set of traditional skills that have been, to some degree, mastered by the artisan.

I think this was a part of the deterioration of physical skills in all the arts. Perhaps the downward slope was keyed by the word *traditional.* It began with painting and the abstract movement. Soon drawing was no longer taught in art school because it was superfluous. "Expression" was all that mattered. As this movement continued and spread, it even became possible to have other people construct your art, based on a concept you provided. It is here that art takes on an intellectual quality that, for me, causes it to lose its sensual, tactile, and visual interest, just in the way that most modern academic music no longer appeals to the ear, but only to the mind. You might as well sit down and read the score, rather than listen to it.

The effect of these trends in writing has been to devalue the basic skills as well. It became all about freedom, as if we can conjure the writer's art from nothing and the process will still work. At this point I probably sound like someone from the Middle Ages, a member of the "craft guilds," the precursors of today's labor unions, whose purpose was to instruct apprentices in the old skills and traditions, and to maintain those skills at a high standard. Indeed, many terms I think about all the time now were never mentioned when I was in college, as if their relevance had somehow been cancelled at midcentury. Here are a few I would've had to look up because they were so unfamiliar: target reader, movement, sentence structure, action—show rather then tell, ending a chapter and providing a hook, flashbacks, voice, character, revision, and plot. There are many more on this list, because literally *nothing* about the craft was ever mentioned to me, although some critical comments did appear in the margins of papers we submitted. Did Dr. Jones assume, that at the age of twenty, we were all so wise in writing lore that he could gloss over it? Ignore it? At this point, I can't speculate on his reasons.

These two trends, I believe, provide the explanation for why I was taught nothing useful. No surprise then, that shortly after graduation, I crashed and burned with a fierce white light, like either a supernova or a white dwarf. Judging from my accomplishment to that point, it must have been the dwarf that gave up the ghost. After all the times I'd been told what a brilliant writer I was, I realized I didn't have what it took to make a good book, so rather than using other means to learn the craft and continue with my dream, I gave up. Although it seemed logical at the moment, that was the mistake of a lifetime.

I blame no one beyond myself. Any artist must own his particular journey or he learns nothing, and therefore fails to grow. If he blames others, he becomes no wiser about people or himself. The process ends, and writing, like any art, needs to be an ongoing development or it dies.

Building a book requires detailed design and construction skills, just as building a house does. To lay the foundation without having them guarantees a disaster. It may look like a house for a while, but eventually it will collapse.

What about people who have a natural talent or a knack for writing? Aren't they immune from this risk? After all, they already speak the language, so why can't they simply write the words down?

This is an exact description of my condition as I emerged from college. I definitely had the knack and a certain flair for words, but without the tools of the trade, I was doomed to failure. Ultimately I resurrected my shattered dream and breathed life into it again. In terms if that long, painful experience, I'd have to say that the greatest credential, and the only one I find meaningful, is having done the work. It's possible that with a skillful instructor this can happen in an academic setting, but when it doesn't, many other ways are available to approach it. You are holding one in your hands. None are shortcuts. All require practice, determination, and the ability to reflect on what you've done and how to improve it.

28.

WRITER'S WORK GROUPS

Over the years I've belonged to a number of different work groups. I've never tried one where the task at every meeting is to spontaneously write for some specified interval on a dictated subject that you're not prepared for, but I can see the use of that as an exercise if you need to loosen up.

Formats vary for the type of meeting I prefer, but basically I got together with several other writers at scheduled intervals. A group of four people makes for a realistic minimum and any number over eight is too many. Five or six is ideal. Bigger groups result in longer meetings where people start to lose focus. All the members will either have previously read a piece from each writer before they arrive, or everyone will be reading from their work at the meeting. Another option is to have the piece read aloud by a member who didn't write it. This allows the author to hear how it sounds in another person's voice, which can be highly instructive. For example, if the reader stumbles repeatedly, that may suggest that the work needs help with the way it flows. If the tone of the writing style doesn't match the content, this is an easy way to spot that.

Each member then critiques the work of the others, usually in a group discussion. Other formats exist with more structure, but I question the need to have the rules more defined than this. Some, for example, would forbid the writer to respond during the group discussion. I don't agree with this, even though I understand that the reason is too prevent the writer from defending himself. The cost is that the writer may not draw out a critic to get more deeply into an interesting point. What is also lost under this limitation can often be a lively exchange that may get into the nuance of the passage more than when the writer is held mute. Exploration of a given comment may be required to make it more usable to the writer, which is, after all, the point.

In a general way, I find groups like this to be quite valuable, but not invariably. I'm a strong believer in test marketing my work, in getting it out there to sophisticated readers for their comments. I have done this since my first book. By sophisticated reader I mean someone who reads in volume and has informed opinions on what she's read. If she feels a passage isn't working, she can explain why, or suggest what might improve it. I also send my finished manuscripts out to people I know for their input on a one-to-one basis.

Some writers fear that exposing their manuscript in progress to a work group will dissipate their ideas and cause the project to lose momentum. I don't have an answer for this. If that happens, then you may have to keep your work under wraps until you've got it all down on paper. You're going to miss out on some free constructive help, but it won't be worth the cost of having your book run aground. In this case, it might be useful to realize that each writer in the group is in the same position of vulnerability. There is a danger to being too thin-skinned in writing. Once your book is published, some people will want to take a shot at you simply from envy. When you're in the public eye, you cannot hide. Being a published writer will toughen you up.

The potential benefits of a gathering like this are many. You will see people's reaction to your piece at a stage when it can still be repaired, rather than in a one-star review on Amazon after publication. If a passage or an idea displeases the majority of the group, particularly when several raise the issue independently, then it's likely to need more work. Naturally, you will always want to measure the comments you receive against your own instincts, which as a rule are truer and more engaged than anyone else's, but listening to other people can be a great help. I once removed a major character from a book after I was more than fifty pages into it. Here is an indicator to use: if you have harbored an unvoiced suspicion that some feature of your book is not working, but you can't bring yourself to confront it, you will be forced to face it when others underline the problem for you. This was what happened to me, and as painful as that was, I did what I needed to do. As a result, for a replacement, I came up with the strongest character in the book. It did not escape me, however, that I needed to be prodded in order to do it.

Another forewarning about passages that need work occurs when you are reading through what you've written and you come to a part you skip over, or rush through as if you took no pleasure in it. This is a clear warning that you have a problem. Don't ignore it—rework that passage or take it out entirely.

Most writers see the work group as a place to get valuable feedback. It is that, but this help occurs in varying degrees of usefulness. About seventy percent of it is in the finer detail: errors of fact, skipped words, misspellings or punctuation issues. This is helpful, but not life changing. After that come whole lines that don't work and paragraphs that read like a billboard, featuring stilted dialog that no one would ever say. Removing or rewriting these is more useful.

At the top, the biggest reason that you came to these meetings at all, is that another member might say something like this: if you had introduced this character at the beginning of the third chapter, instead of in the first, the groundwork would've been prepared, and the impact ten times as great. Or this: if the guy's wife had been killed in the accident instead of his child, then the dynamic of caring for the child and her needs would have both amplified and tempered his response to the crisis he faced as the survivor. It would've added that tension to everything he did. As it is, he sits around mourning the dead child and nothing in the story moves. The narrative has disappeared inside his head.

Even when they require a major alteration, comments like this are game changers in your favor. You didn't see them as you planned and worked on the book, but now you do. Doors open, and the way you look at your story has taken a great leap forward. You realize that it was the hope of getting some feedback of this magnitude that prompted you to join the group to begin with.

One other feature, almost as important, is less obvious, and people coming into a group for the first time rarely realize it. It is that you will be required to produce honest critiques yourself of the work from all the other writers present. Some of them will be involved in genres different from yours and what you're accustomed to reading. Your goal is to produce comments as meaningful to them as the best ones you've received. This will force you to understand the structure and requirements of other forms of writing, which is always useful in understanding your own, if only by reflection or contrast.

The ability to deliver a critique in a style both appropriate and helpful to the other writer is also an exercise in a new kind of expression that will help your work. It provides valuable experience in the task of stepping back from a written piece, one you can usefully apply with your own manuscript.

Another benefit is that the group provides valuable experience in taking criticism. You are not writing for everyone—remember your target reader? Some people will not be moved by your work, no matter how good it is. But the ability to listen carefully to what is being said is critical in learning from it. If you find yourself defending your piece, then you are not hearing the critical comments. It's like putting up a wall of white noise inside your own head. Your job is only to absorb what is said and see if it is helpful to your purpose. If it isn't, or you think it is based on a misunderstanding of your work, then smile and nod as you forget it. No other response is required.

In setting up a group, some care in selection will pay off. Can everyone produce enough to contribute to each session? A member's occasional failure to come up with enough new material for a meeting is not serious, but in general, everyone should have something ready for each gathering, which should be spaced far enough apart to allow for this. People don't write at the same speed, but the members of your group should be serious about writing and able to make that commitment.

Certain types of personalities will be toxic in a group like this, and can undermine the potential benefits. You are depending on people to behave in an honest and helpful way, so a writer who dumps on everyone else's work to elevate his own is not going to be useful to anyone, least of all himself. These people exist and will come forward to join because they like to feel superior to other writers, so be on your guard, and don't hesitate to ask someone to leave if that kind of situation develops. If they have been acting like this it will usually mean they are compensating for the fact that their work is not worth much anyway. You are not there to be kind to fools, only to improve your work and that of your fellow group members who share your degree of seriousness.

Another personality to avoid is one in love with rules. In their deep need for structure, people with that mindset can often demand that the entire group abide by their sense of which presentation and discussion procedures ought to be observed. Writing, however, always needs in some degree to be an experimental process for each of us. We are explorers of ourselves and of our characters as they develop on the page. It is only by probing old boundaries that we break out in new directions, and we ought not to accept the dictates of rigid thinkers, whose greater need for order suggests they are likely to be more fearful than we are, and more than we want or need to be. The best atmosphere for the group is one that encourages creativity and flexibility. It needs to be more exciting than it is careful.

Another hazard to avoid is party or gender politics of any kind, which I regard as an amusement for the light-minded in this kind of setting. First of all, any book that is political is not likely to be relevant for long. Issues of the moment are only that—they change constantly. Second, politics should never be a basis for criticism if the book is not itself political.

Here is a difficult truth: I think that in general the writing world, including fellow writers, coaches and instructors, writer's conferences, editors and publishers, is not the elevated, mutually support-ive environment that I once imagined and hoped it was. Don't look for Shangri-La in this part of the universe. The tenth of my mysteries, titled *The Book Doctor*, is the first of that series to deal with the world of writing, and it plays out in a writer's conference terrain populated by wannabes and false gurus, as well as unscrupulous predators. The population of hopeful writers is a vulnerable group. It resembles a congregation that desperately wants to go to heav-en. They can therefore be told anything that sounds promising of that end, and they will accept it with rapture. If you have lingered at the edges of this world for a while, you will easily recognize some of the players.

The most important thing is to see your-self and the others in the group as working crafts-people. You should have no great pretense about the nobility or elegance of what you're doing. Let the gilded literati stay on the sidelines where they belong.

In my experience, they give real working writers little respect. The members of a functional group need to be helpful and supportive of each other. Be relaxed in the face of hearing comments that may not be what you expected. This is good, because it can raise issues you never thought of.

Writer's work groups thrive best in blue-collar territory. You should expect to sweat and get your hands dirty—after all, you are there to work. Just don't let it show on the page.

29.

WRITER'S CONFERENCES

If you are near the launching of your writing career it's possible that you've never attended a writer's conference. The name sounds faintly intimidating, as if you need a credential, and you're not yet ready to walk up to someone you've never met before and announce that you're a writer too. You know that the response will be, *and what have you written?*

What happens at these events? Formats will vary, but a conference is usually a gathering over three or four days in an attractive climate and setting where more or less established writers offer keynote speeches, group sessions, and sometimes, individual access for the attendees, as at book signings when you can say a few words to your favorite author. Less established writers offer sessions focused on subjects like character development, plot, dialog, pitching to an agent, and other valuable aspects of the writer's work skills. Often in view will be an agent or two, offering pitch sessions. Here you submit a sample of your project and get his reaction. You will find coaches of various types working the crowd, looking for talented writers to polish into possible success stories, and some may be presenters themselves, largely talking about how tough it is to break into New York (without their help). Some conferences, but not all, will offer a session on self-publishing and e-books, often without many specific details.

In my experience most of these conferences are still aligned with the old way of publishing and marketing, so don't expect much emphasis on self-publishing tips. The reason for this is that beginning writers typically define success as being published in New York in the traditional way. It is the sensation of running their index fingers down the spine of that first novel as it stands proudly on the shelf of a bookstore in midtown Manhattan. This, however, will inevitably change over time. Recently, success in writing has grown larger than this image, which is taking on an increasingly Norman Rockwell flavored nostalgia.

Let's take a step back and look at the mechanics of the conference process from the faculty point of view. All the writers in the position of presenters, from the most glamorous down to the barely relevant, are attending to promote their books.

Usually a small, improvised bookstore is attached where attendees and the public can buy them. Often the most successful authors will schedule autograph sessions. The highest-ranking presenter, usually giving the keynote address, will most likely be paid a stipend and have her expenses covered too. At a recent conference I have seen 150 copies of her book be snapped up. The others may have subsidies or other assistance with their expenses, such as lodging in the homes of local unpaid volunteers.

Do not confuse this format with residencies, where longer term housing is offered for an extended set period, with or without some improving sessions, as a way of providing isolation and calm for people with a project going, who, because of family or job commitments, have a tough time gaining access to their own thought processes and a laptop simultaneously. Old mansions in the country with cabins scattered through the adjacent woods are a typical venue for this.

This sounds good so far, and it is, if we don't demand more than it's capable of delivering.

The first issue to examine is the faculty selection process, which, with the exception of some academic conferences where an English Department staff is the core faculty, is opaque to the public.

Who vets these people to be presenters? Often their qualifications, aside from the star presenter, consists of their availability in the required time frame, having a book to promote so that they're willing to work for free, and their association with a clique or insider group that uses them again and again because they are kindred spirits, and the conference management knows what to expect from them. This does not mean their presentations are always good. I would suggest, having attended a number of different conferences, that their ability to provide usable content to the attendees is appropriately open to question. Nonetheless, some may be valuable, even extraordinarily so. Occasionally, when the chemistry and content is right, you may be inspired by one of these presentations.

Often the attendee's response to presenters is geared to his level of sophistication. What I'm suggesting is that their performance is so uneven that it's something of a crapshoot. Moderate your expectations and listen carefully as you take notes. As always, the value of what anyone suggests to you, even in *these* pages, as I noted in the Introduction, depends on how well those suggestions fit and enhance *your* process. You are the writing information consumer, and no godlike person possesses the key to make every amateur into a strong writer. Mingling with established writers may feel great, but if you do attend a conference, don't loose sight of the fact that taking your skills to the next level is the principal reason you're in attendance.

An ancillary benefit for all this imported talent is the awestruck sheen in the attendees' eyes as they look at the upper level of presenters.

Now that we know what the staff is getting out of this, let's examine the benefits to the attendees.

Even without my prompting, you already knew that writing is a solitary task, where the results go untested for long periods, and the writer is open to constant doubt about whether any of his efforts will ever prove to be meaningful, even to himself. Will they ever see daylight? At times he envisions a charitable relative stuffing the eight spiral-bound volumes of his unpublished manuscripts into the coffin next to his stiffened elbow prior to closing the lid.

No conference that I've looked at, other than those with residency formats, has a qualifying feature where you have to prove your worthiness to attend. You submit nothing but your credit card or check; either will be a sufficient credential. Does this mean that management doesn't care if you can write? Draw your own conclusion; after all, who is caring now? Management's chief interest is that you *attend*. Increasingly, some conferences are being billed as designed for readers too. An economy of scale can be achieved by pumping up the numbers, and the conference promoters are well aware of it.

I don't mean to appear cynical about this, because I'm not. I regard this chapter as realistic. But these conferences, for profit or not, are businesses above anything else, and to get the most value from them, it's important not to glamorize what they do simply because by attending you find yourself in the midst of a supportive crowd that shares your ambitions even as you rub shoulders with real writers who seem to illustrate that it can actually be done.

For you, whether the novice, the moderately experienced, or the wannabe writer who's trying to find a way to get started, what goes on there that most makes the experience of this kind of literary gathering worthwhile?

The first benefit is that this assembled group is a community of equals, at least in terms of hopefulness. As you write in your attic, at the breakfast table before anyone else gets up, or in your guest bedroom at home when everyone else is in bed, no one stands up and surrounds you to cheer you on. No one offers you a high five as you shut down your laptop or cap your pen after a productive session. No one even asks what you're writing about, or if they do, the next two questions would be, what? Why? Hasn't Aunt Alice been dead for ages, so who cares if you base a novel on her life for nineteen years as a blind missionary in Honduras?

But in the halls of this conference, the hungry crowd looks much like you. Their mouths are never quite closed all the way, as if they could start breathing heavily at a moment's notice. Is that a famous author over there? *Isn't that guy somebody we should know?* He sure looks a lot younger on his book cover. In the discussion sessions, the participants display that same tentative engagement with the important issues of literature that no one else in your life cares a damn about. At home, your occasional question about what is happening now in the world of pronouns was always met with a wall of blank stares. Like you, the people around you now want some real answers, and you realize that even when almost no one else in the known world seems to care, these questions still matter deeply to them too. You also suspect that some of these people can't quite afford to be in this sun-drenched enclave in Costa Rica or Arizona, but after all, it's still winter in Escanaba, and that's where winter really *means* something.

All around you, the atmosphere is saturated with books and the urgent talk of books. In the improvised bookshop attached to the conference, every presenter is represented, as well as some you haven't heard of. You start to feel that your writing effort, which has gotten little support from the people around you at home, may really be worth something after all. It is as if you have stumbled through an unlocked door and found yourself in the midst of a congregation full of people embracing your own obscure religion, speaking not in tongues, but in actual, suddenly meaningful, words. It makes what you are trying to do suddenly seem more possible than you ever imagined.

This fabric of collective engagement, even of enthusiasm, is one of the benefits you will receive from a writer's conference. For a few days you will wear it like a glowing mantle that shields you from the massed indifference you have observed too often in the outside world. This may even be the principal benefit to be had in a conference like this. It is one of the few times in your life when you can feel that being a writer makes you part of a movement that possesses both velocity and momentum. It will be the only time your solitary task seems inevitable, rather than staggeringly haphazard. Take it in with all your senses and relish it, because by the time you are back on the plane going home, a faint glow is all that will remain to sustain you.

The small-scale sessions can be helpful. Take notes and retain the handouts. When permitted, ask questions related to specific issues you are facing *in your own book or writing style*. These are the questions you could not bring up at the end of the keynote address, where only issues of general interest were allowed. Obtaining detailed, useful information that will stay with you is more important than the keynote address, even though it doesn't feel as impressive because these lesser sessions are usually fronted by no famous faces.

The big players at this or any conference are not there to give you concrete assistance in their speeches. They are present to play their star roles and to thrill you with their aura. Their task is to appear lovable and talented to the audience so that you will buy their books, and like newbie evangelists, spread the word about how great they were to see in person. Enjoy this for what it is, but six months from now do not expect to remember any of what they said. They rarely talk about writing as a craft, the single element that would be most useful to you, and to everybody else in the audience.

The measure of what lasting value you take away from any conference is this: what are you still using from it six months later? Did it change any of your existing habits or get you started on new ones? Did it guide you through or around any roadblocks? Did you gain any insights about character or plot that strengthened your writing? Was the ease with which you can access your own author's voice enhanced by being there? Did you meet a new contact that might help you get published? In short, can you characterize any of your conference experiences as a breakthrough?

When I walked through this review process myself, when I added up the net improvement I received from session presenters and keynote speakers over the five conferences I'd attended over several years, I stopped attending them. I had received some minor benefits, but none that changed my approach in any meaningful or lasting way.

Overall, for me the chief benefit was that sense of collective engagement I mentioned above. Do not underestimate its value, because it does have merit in an occupation so solitary, so isolated and greeted with indifference. One way to nurture that effect is to make friends with as many fellow writers as you can at a conference. Talk especially to attendees who work in your own genre with whom you can maintain contact by email or phone after the conference. This will, in a small way, extend that feeling of community that is so hard to find among writers.

The question remains of how to choose a conference. Search *choosing a writers conference* and you'll find enough resources to explore. Refine the process down to those that are a good fit for your kind of writing. I'm inclined to believe that attending at least one conference is good for most writers. Whether you need more after that depends on how much you're getting out of it. Measure it against your costs.

As writers we must be observers first. Use your powers of observation to understand what you're looking at and how it works. This will make you a more realistic participant in the conference you've chosen, and you'll avoid disappointment at the outcome.

The websites below, along with much other valuable information about the writer's world, both provide long lists of conferences, mostly in the US and Canada, but international as well.

Poets and Writers: www.pw.org/conferences and residencies.

Also: www.newpages.com/writing-conferences/.

30.

WHY TRY?

At first I had intended to place this chapter near the beginning of the book, which is when I wrote it. Knowing the reasons for starting a project as massive and committed as writing a book seemed like a reasonable place to begin. Later, I thought that anyone who had read this far must be more serious than those who had not, and it properly belonged at the end. Anyone who has reached this chapter has absorbed many of my suggestions and whether he plans to use them or not, this looks like a proper time to step back and examine the general concept of writing a book. Why do it at all? Is it right for anyone who merely has the whim to be an author? Can the required drive and focus be generated within the filmy boundaries of the average daydream?

In many ways the reasons for taking a serious run at writing and publishing a book are not different from any other creative endeavor. You must be passionate about that idea to have processed all this material and still be thinking about it. It requires being a thoughtful reader yourself and able to understand what you're looking at on another author's page. Writers are first of all readers. Finally, you must have a genuine *need* to do it, knowing that it will compliment your life in ways that nothing else can. Not doing it would diminish you. If this does not describe you, how did you come this far? (unless you're a reviewer.)

The possibility of becoming a good and skillful writer is something you can approach through study, insight, and hard work. *Determination* and *persistence* are the keys. The odds of becoming a famous writer are still remote; we can acknowledge that. However, if you don't take a run at it, your chances are effectively zero. You will have guaranteed that you have no possibility at all of success. This is not a technique widely used by winners in any field.

When I finish a book, and the one you're reading now is my nineteenth, in addition to the two I burned back in the late sixties, I am always disappointed. Not that the book has turned out to be less than I'd hoped for, (although that has happened), it's that I had such a great time writing it that I didn't want the journey to end. Many people have said this, and it's also one of my core beliefs: it is truly the journey, and not the destination, that is most meaningful.

If you're a person who marks up books, underline the following paragraph:

If you take a run at it and fall short of success, however you define that, you will still have *nothing* to reproach yourself with. You will know you gave it your best effort, and you will have had the best part of it, which is the writing of *your* book, a book that could not have been written by anyone else in the world. That achievement is in itself unique, and no one can take it from you.

If, however, you make excuses for not working, or you're frightened or just plain put off by the level of effort required, or discouraged by the tiny likelihood of success in the marketplace, then you will always be plagued by the fact that you will never know what would have happened if you had made your best effort. You will have sold yourself and your dream short, receiving nothing but a more average life in return. A bad bargain indeed, and again, not the act of a winner in any field.

Above all else, keep this thought in mind: you cannot lose by writing your book, only by *not* writing it. Fame and financial success are the smallest parts of what a dedicated writer may receive for his efforts. Even if your book does not achieve great sales, you will have still found an audience, one that cares about what you have to say. Even for the bestselling novelist, the *most* rewarding part is his journey, just as it is for you. That is the equalizer between you and the mighty, and it is also the best possible bottom line.

Go for it!